THE DRAGON ROARS

For three months, unabated violence had rained down upon Hong Kong. At the Eastern Police Division, Superintendent Jack Barratt faced the almost impossible task of keeping the rioters under control. Then a young Lieutenant of the U.S. Navy was seduced by a bar girl in Wanchai, and suddenly Barratt had the break that might lead him to at least one of the main Communist subversion centres. The problem was to keep his leads alive.

Books by Charles Leader
in the Linford Mystery Library:

A WREATH OF POPPIES
A WREATH FOR MISS WONG
A WREATH FROM BANGKOK
A WREATH OF CHERRY BLOSSOM
THE DOUBLE M MAN
KINGDOM OF DARKNESS
DEATH OF A MARINE
SALESMAN OF DEATH
SCAVENGERS OF WAR

CHARLES LEADER

THE DRAGON ROARS

Complete and Unabridged

LINFORD
Leicester

First published in Great Britain

First Linford Edition
published 1997

British Library CIP Data

Leader, Charles, *1938*–
     The dragon roars.—Large print ed.—
Linford mystery library
1. Detective and mystery stories
2. Large type books
I. Title
823.9′14 [F]

ISBN 0–7089–5074–4

Published by
F. A. Thorpe (Publishing) Ltd.
Anstey, Leicestershire

Set by Words & Graphics Ltd.
Anstey, Leicestershire
Printed and bound in Great Britain by
T. J. International Ltd., Padstow, Cornwall

This book is printed on acid-free paper

1

Border Post

ON their side of the border the Chinese machine-gunners assembled their weapons with deft precision, setting them up to cover the British police post and government building at the frontier village of Sha Tau Kok. The massed Red Guards, shallow youths revelling in the first brute flush of their man-strength, were being whipped into a frenzy by the older, professionally-schooled agitators from Canton. They howled their Mao slogans, and thoughts from the little red book that was their distorted bible, thrusting their fists on high to display proudly the red arm bands just above their elbows. They were like a dangerous flock of screaming, young-human parrots, and perhaps

1

more dangerous than the trained party men with their automatic weapons. The party men, like the frontier guards with the machine-guns, had discipline, but the Red Guards were as ill-controlled as a river. They could be directed, but not stopped.

Inside the police post the Chinese constables waited tensely. The garrison at Sha Tau Kok numbered approximately one-hundred and sixty-five men, under the command of an English Superintendent. About half of them were barricaded inside the police post itself, while the remainder had taken refuge in the government building some fifty yards behind. They were well armed with carbines, standard .38 police revolvers, and the special riot guns that fired either tear gas or eight-inch wooden bullets that could effectively stop a mob if ricocheted off the ground at knee height. However, this time the mob that faced them across the street of the divided village was a thousand strong, and the carbines and the riot guns were heavily outweighed by the machine-guns that had now been brought into position.

Superintendent Ralph Nichols decided that he had watched the preparations for long enough. He didn't need the experience of twenty-three years as a Colonial police officer to tell him that this crowd meant business. The massed, yelling clamour that faced them was nearing fever pitch and a decision had to be made. He turned to the stiff-faced Chinese Inspector beside him and said grimly:

"Ling, order three rounds of tear gas fired, disperse those gunners round that first machine-gun."

Ling nodded briskly, and automatically drew his revolver clear of its black leather holster as he turned to relay the order.

★ ★ ★

In a concealed gulley three-quarters of a mile away Lee Kung was just a little

3

too distant to hear the muffled crunch as the tear gas shells exploded, but he heard clearly the angry chattering of the machine-gun that followed. The roar of the mob reached him too, and the crackle of smaller automatic weapons, and he knew that the attack upon the border post had burst into flower. He stood up from the rock on which he had been sitting and spoke sharply to the young peasant girl standing a few yards away who was staring nervously towards the sounds of battle. She turned to face him and he indicated with a nodding jerk of his head that it was time for them to go.

The girl moved past him and he knew that she was afraid of him. But that was good. It was right that the masses should have the respect of fear for a senior member of the party. He called her 'comrade', but they both knew that they were on very different levels of the party structure. There were many intonations that could be used to utter the simple word 'comrade', and Lee Kung knew them all.

He was a tall man, for he had been born in the northern province of Shantung where men were bred taller and tougher than the Chinese of the south. He despised these flimsy southerners, and was ill-pleased that he had been sent from Peking to Canton to work amongst them. He was even less pleased with his present task which necessitated a surreptitious entry into Hong Kong, and his flat nose wrinkled with disgust when the girl stopped and pointed out the brickwork entrance to the sewer culvert that passed beneath the border.

A muffled uproar and the sound of wild shooting still came from the besieged village of Sha Tau Kok, rolling over the low, intervening hill. The mob was occupying the attention of every constable of the Frontier Emergency Control Unit along this section of the border, and Lee Kung was tempted to walk boldly upright into the so-called

New Territories of the imperialist colony. It was undignified for a senior party member to crawl through a sewer to reach territory that was part of China, and rightfully belonged to the People's Republic. However, his instructions had said explicitly that he was to be guided through the sewer to make absolutely sure that he was not seen, and instructions from the party were not flexible. Lee Kung hesitated only for a moment, and then inclined his head in a curt gesture for the girl to lead on. He did not address her by name, for although they had been briefly introduced he had already forgotten her name. She was just a tool to be used and her name was not important.

The girl stepped down into the narrow gulley, hoisting up her grey skirts as she paddled into the ankle deep dirty water. Lee Kung started to follow her, hesitated, and then removed his canvas shoes. The girl had ducked into the low brick tunnel, and then turned with her peasant's hat scraping dirt and dust from the arched roof. Lee Kung rolled the trouser legs of his faded blue peasant suit up to his knees, and then made another impatient gesture to urge her forward. Already he found the smell of the sewer distasteful, and he grimaced again as he placed his bare feet into the water. The girl's feet were already bare, for she possessed no shoes at all. She led the way, blotting out most of the light from the far end of the tunnel with her hunched figure. Lee Kung groped his way behind her, cursing silently as the stink got worse and the foul water became deeper. He too wore a wide straw hat that scraped the brickwork above his head and brought pats of dirt and damp mould falling on to his shoulders. The girl waded easily ahead, but Lee Kung was cramped and bent almost double and his shoulders began to ache. The sound of the distant battle was shut out after they had penetrated the first few yards, and there was silence but for the girl's breathing and their own splashings.

Lee Kung tried to forget that he was crawling through a sewer, and cast his mind ahead to the job he had been sent to do. For three months past the Communist organizers in Hong Kong had been stirring up anti-British feeling, creating demonstrations, riots and strikes with all the fervour they could muster, but so far they had failed to repeat the success of their counterparts in Macao, the Portuguese colony on the opposite side of the great estuary of the Pearl River. In Macao the imperialists had opened fire to kill seven demonstrators, and had then been forced to humbly apologize and admit their brutality to the world by the massed invasion threat of thousands of the Red Guards. Macao's humiliation had been achieved. It had been demonstrated to the world that Macao could only exist with the consent of China. Peking had decreed that similar events should occur in Hong

Kong, proving to the world that the British were no better than the Portugese, and that they too could exist only if they bowed to the will of mighty China.

Somehow the plan had miscarried, and the pattern had not been repeated. A minor dispute at a plastic flower company had enabled the trade unions to stage the first strike and begin the surge of riots and violence, but despite all provocation the British-controlled police forces had so far restrained from killing any of the demonstrators. The overall success of the operations demanded martyrs to prove the brutality of the imperialists, but so far the imperialists had refused to take lives. Despite the twelve continuous weeks of turmoil and political and industrial disruption, and despite all the efforts of the party organizers and the vast sums of party money issued to pay the agitators and riot-leaders, the desired results had not been obtained. Peking had grown impatient, and in Canton the wall posters had been plastered up in their hundreds demanding that those responsible should be made to account for their failure. To the Chinese mind the victory over Macao had demonstrated that there was no defence for those who failed to achieve victory over Hong Kong. In Canton there was a strong demand that heads should roll, but Peking was divided. To recall the Communist leaders in Hong Kong to confess their failure was to admit that failure. Peking still desired the humiliation of the British Colony, and was willing to give the party men on the spot one final chance to earn atonement. Lee Kung's task was to deliver Peking's ultimatum, to impress Peking's displeasure upon the local organizers, and to spur them into achieving their ordered goal.

Lee Kung was coldly determined that the next wave of violence, which he would help to organize, would not fail. For now the continued failure of the local party officials would be his failure also. The chain of failure passed upward, just as the chain of command passed down, and he too would have to account in Peking. In the soulless party machine there was no cog that was too big to be broken, and only the great Chairman himself was held above criticism.

Sunlight filtered into the underground gloom and they came out of the culvert. Lee Kung straightened his back with an inward sigh of relief, and drew his first deep breath in the last five minutes. The sounds of gunfire were audible again from the direction of Sha Tau Kok, and he wondered whether the dynamite squads had yet blasted their way into the police post. He stared towards the unseen battle for a moment, and then realized that the girl was looking back at him with scared eyes. She was very young, perhaps sixteen or seventeen, and those sharp, piercing eyes were like those of a frightened grey bird beneath the straw edge of her hat. She indicated that they must still keep low, and then crouched her shoulders and began to scuttle away along the narrow drainage ditch. Lee Kung bowed his shoulders reluctantly and began to follow her.

The girl had been born in this part of the New Territories and had lived there all her life. She had helped to till the green paddy fields since the age of six, and she knew every ditch, stone and gulley for miles around. No one saw them as she led the tall party man from Canton away from the frontier line, for most of the peasants had fled the fields and headed wisely for their homes at the first sounds of the disturbance at Sha Tau Kok, but even if they had been seen it was unlikely that anyone would have taken notice of two additional peasants.

After the first half mile Lee Kung straightened his back and ignored the uncertain warnings of his guide. He walked briskly and she hurried along beside him, pointing out the way until eventually they came to an unmade road. Here the girl pulled two ancient bicycles out of a ditch, and they both mounted up and pedalled swiftly away. They came to a main road, and then after another mile to a small village. The girl turned into a tumbledown backyard behind one of the houses where stray chickens scratched and shreds of washing hung from a line between two posts. She scrambled off her cycle, leaned it against one of the posts, and then ran to help the party man dismount. Lee Kung left her to manage the bicycle and moved to meet the young Chinese who had promptly appeared. The young man wore western trousers and a white shirt, and an air of urgency and importance. He greeted the party man with respect, and then led him quickly into the house.

Lee Kung followed the young Chinese up a flight of stairs, ignoring the old Chinese woman who curiously watched him pass. In the room at the top of the stairs there was a suit of cheap western clothes, including a hat and shoes, all laid out for him upon the sagging bed. Lee Kung glanced at them briefly, registering nothing upon his face, and then he crossed to the window where the main road ran below outside.

The young Chinese said tersely:

"There is a car waiting. Comrade Kung. I am to take you into Kowloon as soon as you are ready."

Lee Kung turned, stayed cold long enough to let the self-importance die out of the young man's eyes and then answered:

"We will wait."

★ ★ ★

Thirty minutes passed before the first of the British army trucks roared past along the road below the window. Kung watched and noted the flat, slightly eager faces of the armed soldiers packed closely together in the back of the truck. More trucks swept past, noisily swirling up the dust, but

14

although they were British trucks the soldiers inside were all Asians. Kung knew that these must be the Gurkhas, the mercenary fighters from Nepal with their wicked, heavy kukri knives. The convoy vanished quickly in its haste to relieve the beleaguered police garrison at Sha Tau Kok, and Kung felt a spasm of pure hatred towards the sturdy little hill soldiers from Nepal. They were Asians betraying Asians, and were even lower than the degenerate peoples of the west. He reflected that one day soon the People's Republic of China would have to *liberate* Nepal.

When the last truck was out of sight he turned away from the window. He had changed into the clothes that had been provided for him and the young Chinese was still waiting. The girl, now that her task was over, had made herself invisible in some hidden corner of the house. Lee Kung said coldly:

"Fetch the car. Now we will go."

2

Crude Murder

IN the central office of Eastern Police station on Hong Kong island the telephone rang with a shrill blare. Divisional Superintendent Jack Barratt plucked the receiver deftly from its cradle only slightly faster than was usual, answered with a sharp growl, and then listened intently. Chan, the station's senior Chinese inspector looked up from the second desk in the room and ceased his writing in mid-stroke of his pen. His face was passive as he watched his superior, and there was only a minimum of tension in the rigid hand that hovered with the pen. Barratt's face was craggy and weather-beaten, and just a little more sun-browned than that of the working farmer he might have become if he

16

had stayed to live his life in his native Norfolk. It was a strong face that gave nothing away until its owner was ready, as inscrutable in its own way as those of the Chinese amongst whom he had worked and lived for the past eighteen years. Chan had to wait until the telephone was replaced and Barratt relaxed, and then the Englishman met his enquiring eyes. He said gravely:

"Well, Charles, the Gurkhas have reached Sha Tau Kok. The Army sent six hundred of them to relieve Nichols and his garrison. They had to advance through sniper fire to drive off the mob around the government building. Then they were able to relieve the police post itself without firing another shot. Now the Gurkhas are taking up positions to face the Chinese frontier guards across the border, but the mob itself is scattered. The pressure's off."

Chan knew from Barratt's tone that the news had not been all rosy, and asked in a carefully flat voice:

"What were the casualties?"

"Nichols reported five of his constables killed, and at least twelve wounded. The mob tried to blast their way into the border post with dynamite, but tear gas and the riot guns kept them out. Nichols said that it was bloody rough while it lasted, and that it could have been much worse if the Gurkhas hadn't arrived as quickly as they did." Barratt paused, and then asked bluntly. "What do you make of it, Charles? Is Mao ready to ride the Chinese dragon right into Hong Kong, or is he just having difficulty in hanging on to the reins?"

Chan gave the question some thought, knowing that Barratt was always prepared to wait for a considered answer. The Chinese Inspector was a sturdy man, a little taller than the average Chinese but not exceptionally so. He was thirty-three years of age and a very efficient policeman. He and Barratt worked well together. He had worked his way up through the ranks, and in his early years as a young constable he had been christened 'Charlie' by his colleagues after the famous American detective of fiction. The name had stuck, and was still used behind his back by his juniors, but only Barratt called him 'Charles', which was just as friendly, and more befitting the dignity of a senior inspector. He stared down at the report he had been signing, slowly and automatically completed his name, and then pushed the pen and the sheet of paper aside. He said at last:

"No, Mao does not want to take over Hong Kong. Not at this present time. From China's viewpoint the advantages and disadvantages of a British colony on their doorstep, and of the Portuguese at Macao, are very equally balanced. They may publicly despise us as imperialists and capitalists, but the People's Republic of China is only an empire under another name. The rule of Mao Tse Tung is as absolute as that of Ghengis Khan, and as eager for conquest — look to Mongolia and Tibet! And China is also as conscious of the need for money as the so-called capitalist west. They need foreign exchange, and Hong Kong and Macao are their only sources of that foreign exchange. In nineteen sixty-six China earned one-hundred and seventy-three million pounds through Hong Kong alone, and they cannot afford to throw away an annual income of that size. China complains loudly about the British and American naval vessels using Hong Kong, but there again they have advantages. The ships are all photographed in the harbour, and when the sailors drink and talk in the Wanchai bars any information they may let slip is filtered through to Red China."

Chan paused, searching his mind for any point he might have missed, and then finished:

"Hong Kong and Macao are China's eyes and ears to the world, and China will not cut them off. Chairman Mao will not spite his own face. Hong Kong will be allowed to stay a British Colony, but Mao wishes to impose his own terms. He demands a propaganda victory, a repetition of Macoa, but more than that he wants us cowed, and more strictly subject to China's will."

Barratt frowned, wrinkling his heavy eyebrows, and then said:

"That's in close agreement with my assessment, or at least with my assessment up until this morning. But this attack on Sha Tau Kok is a change in the pattern. Its the first time that the Reds have tried to break through the border, and the first time that we've had men killed. We're a long way south of Peking, and Mao and the party leaders may have lost their grip on the whole situation. Their limited aims don't help us much if they've lost control."

"There is that danger. Today's attack was obviously organized from Canton, and the Red Guards are young dogs who have been allowed to run wild. But it would take the Red Army to invade and occupy Hong Kong, and there Mao does have control. We both know that the Army could march in at any time, but Mao will hold them back."

Barratt nodded and then leaned back in his chair, spreading his broad shoulders and staring thoughtfully up at the white-washed ceiling, thinking aloud:

"Then Sha Tau Kok was just part of the general increasing pressure, probably the trigger for a new wave of riots and protests here and in Kowloon. We'd best be prepared, Charles." Another thought crossed his mind and he added. "It could also have been staged as a cover. It would be interesting to know how many fresh agitators were hurried across the border while our men were pinned down in their own police post."

Chan shrugged carelessly:

"Hong Kong is already filled with paid agitators. A few more or less will not make any real difference to our troubles."

★ ★ ★

Twenty minutes later the telephone rang again, as shrilly and as urgently as before. Chan was bowed over the duty roster and the names of the constables due to make up the riot patrols for that night, and again it was Barratt who lifted the receiver. His mouth hardened as he listened to the call, and then he snapped harshly:

"Stay there, Sergeant. Let no one touch the body, and let no one leave the ship until I arrive."

He slammed the phone down. Chan was attentive.

"More trouble?"

"Bad. On our patch this time. One of our constables has just been killed down in the docks."

Chan's face darkened, and then he reached for his cap and moved swiftly out of the room, shouting a curt order for the desk sergeant to organize a car. Barratt jammed his own cap hard on to his head and followed only a step behind.

Within three minutes they were

seated in the back of a speeding police car, moving west along Connaught Road Central beneath the white, skyscraper blocks of Victoria and the green shoulder of the peak. It was late afternoon and the blue dazzle had faded from the still waters of the harbour, and the lines of small freighters anchored off the numbered buoys were like a flock of patient, rusted ducks. The police driver was cutting deftly through the busy traffic, and many heads were turned among the shuffling streams of pedestrians who mingled along the passing pavement. A few of the flat, Chinese faces were impassive, some were curious, but many, schooled by the goadings and incitements of the past weeks of curfews and violence, reflected sharp hatred. The two men in the car could not hear, but could sense the mutterings and the temper of the crowds. Chan turned his gaze inward and asked the question that was foremost in his mind:

"Who is the dead man?"

"Constable Ho Kin. Apparently there was some trouble aboard one of the ships at Queen's Wharf, a French boat named the *Célérité*. A fight broke out between dockers and the crew. Constable Kin went aboard to sort it out, and was killed in the brawl. Sergeant Fong got there about five minutes later with another Constable and they're standing guard until we get there."

Chan made no more comment, but Barratt knew what he was thinking. Five minutes was sufficient time for the killer to get ashore, and despite the speed with which they were moving he would have time to clear the area before the cordon they had ordered was in position. There were hundreds of paid thugs and hooligans at present roaming Hong Kong, and their chances of tracking down the man they wanted would be slim.

It took them ten minutes to reach the wharf. The Colony's main docks were on Kowloon side behind the long, ultra-modern Ocean Terminal where the giant cruise liners docked, and here there were only a few small tramps. The *Célérité* was badly named, for she was worn and smoke-grimed, and obviously slow. She was a high-bridged vessel of eight hundred tons, lying close to the quayside where the still derricks of the dockside cranes hung motionless over her opened holds. The name of her home port, *Marseilles*, was only just readable on her rusted stern. There was a small group of Chinese in grimy sweat shirts or overalls clustered around the steel leg of one of the cranes, but all work had stopped. They began to jabber quickly as the police car roared to a stop close by the ship's gangway, but then fell silent again as Barratt and Chan scrambled out.

Barratt led the way up the gangway, feeling it sway and creak under his fourteen-stone weight. A constable in a peaked cap and the stiffly starched shirt and shorts of the Hong Kong police appeared above them and saluted smartly. His face was a blank mask that might also have been starched as he reported:

"Nobody has left the ship, Superintendent. Sergeant Fong is waiting for you in the forward hold."

Barratt nodded briefly and told the man to stay at his post. He hurried past with Chan, and neither of them looked back to the quayside as more police cars appeared and began spilling uniformed men out on to the wharf. The area would be searched, but they both knew that the dragnet would only scoop up the curious bystanders who had nothing on their conscience. They passed through the starboard side alley and came out on to the foredeck where a group of Chinese seamen were standing nervously close by the open hold. Three of the ship's French officers were also present, a junior officer, and the ship's Captain and First Mate, all easily recognizable by the gold rings on the sleeves of their dark blue jackets.

The Captain stepped forward, he was a dark-faced man in his fifties who wore a neat gallic beard. His face showed regret, mixed with a small amount of annoyance and irritability.

"This is a terrible thing, *Messieurs*. Especially that it should happen aboard my ship. I am Captain Raymond Tellier, and this is *Monsieur* Lombard, my Chief Officer."

Barratt acknowledged both men, while Chan moved past behind him and began to descend swiftly into the open hold. Barratt glanced briefly at the waiting group of Chinese and the third officer as he introduced himself, and then asked briskly:

"Exactly what did happen here, Captain? I only know that one of my men has been killed down in the hold."

The Frenchman shrugged, an indication that he too did not know all the details.

"There was trouble, soon after we start unloading. Some kind of dispute

28

between my seamen and the dock workers who come aboard. There is a big argument on the quayside. The constable comes and then a fight breaks out down there in the hold. The constable comes aboard and goes down there. The next thing there is much shouting and everybody runs out of the hold. The constable stays behind because he is dead."

"Who was on deck at the time in charge of the unloading, yourself, or Monsieur Lombard?"

"Neither of us." The Chief Officer spoke up suddenly. "I was ashore at the time. I left the ship's Third Officer in charge of the deck. When I returned to the ship everything was all over. The Chinese were all running away. I came aboard with your Sergeant who was running to the scene, but we were both a little too late."

Tellier had signalled the younger officer to come over and join them, and introduced him briefly.

"This is Monsieur Jean Durdent, my

Third Officer. He was the only officer on deck."

Durdent was barely out of his teens, a slim, pale-faced boy who stood stiffly with his shoulders braced back. Barratt was in no mood for smiling, but he made the effort to relax his face slightly to put the boy at his ease. Then his glance rested on Tellier again.

"Where were you, Captain, while all this was happening?"

"I was in my cabin, Monsieur, asleep."

Barratt raised his heavy eyebrows.

"Through a brawl and a riot. There must have been a lot of noise?"

"There was." Tellier spoke sharply, resenting the implied rebuke. "But I spent most of last night on the bridge of my ship, the *Célérité* docked here in Hong Kong shortly after daybreak, and it has been a very busy morning. There is always noise when a ship unloads, there are always squabbles, and the Chinese are a naturally noisy people. I was tired and I tried to ignore the noise as usual." He paused, and then added curtly. "Naturally I was not aware that my Chief Officer had been called ashore and that Monsieur Durdent was alone in charge of the deck."

Barratt felt no urge to press that particular issue any further. During the past three months he had spent too many sleepless nights of his own on riot patrol to feel any hostility towards a man who had to catch his sleep when the opportunity provided. Instead he turned to the ship's Third Officer.

"Then perhaps you will tell me exactly what you saw happen?"

Durdent nodded. His English was an effort and he said haltingly:

"It is as the Captain has said. There was trouble when the dock workers come aboard to start the unloading. They start to quarrel with our seamen around the hold. They are talking angrily all the time. They start to work and go down into the hold, but then they stop and start to talk angrily again. It is the dock workers, I think, they are trying to — to stir up trouble."

"What was it all about? What were they saying?"

Durdent looked apologetic. "I don't know, Monsieur. I do not understand the Chinese. I only know they argue. Then it seems that everybody is arguing, and talking all at once. The men on the deck of the *Célérité* they argue with the men in the hold, and with the men on the quay. The crane stops working and a crowd gathers on the quay. The policeman comes to the crowd on the quay and tries to talk to them, but they are shouting at him and will not listen. I think that perhaps I should call Captain Tellier, but I knew that he has been awake all night — "

Durdent hesitated, and Barratt guessed that he had been afraid of his Captain's irritable temper. Tellier said nothing, and Barratt prompted the younger man along.

"What happened then?"

"The fight broke out in the hold. There were perhaps a dozen men down there, perhaps more, all of them fighting amongst the cargo. I shouted down for them to stop but they would not obey me. Then I called down to the policeman. I thought that perhaps he could stop them. He could speak to them in Chinese. He came aboard very quickly and he too shouted down in the hold for them to stop. He drew his revolver but they ignored him also. Then he started to climb down into the hold to stop them. I told him to wait, but he would not, so then I decided that I would have to wake the Captain."

"You left the constable to go into the hold alone?"

Durdent looked wretched. "I told him to wait," he repeated. "I hurried towards the bridge to find Captain Tellier. Then there was much shouting behind me. I looked back to see that the Chinese were all climbing out of the hold and running away. They run down

33

the gangway, and then I see Monsieur Lombard with the police sergeant and another policeman running fast across the quay towards the ship. I decide not to wake the Captain after all. I wait for Monsieur Lombard, and then we go back with the two policemen to the hold."

He stopped there, and the First Officer filled in the rest.

"I climbed down into the hold with your sergeant. Only the constable was there. He was lying dead across some bales of raw wool. The only men left on deck were members of our own Chinese crew. I questioned them with the help of the ship's bo'sun. They say that it was the dock workers who attacked the constable, and that they all ran ashore after he was killed."

Tellier added the final word.

"Monsieur Lombard then called me from my bunk. I co-operated with your sergeant and since then no one has been allowed to leave this ship."

Barratt tried hard to stop his face

34

from turning sour, resisting the impulse to remark that any fool could lock an empty stable door. Instead he thanked the three men briefly, and then requested them to wait while he descended into the hold.

Sergeant Fong was waiting for him in the gloom at the bottom of the steel-runged ladder. The sergeant was an older man who had guided many young constables through their formative years, and in the half darkness his face looked sallow and grey. He said nothing, but pointed to the spot where Chan was standing over the crumpled body. Barratt stared at him hard in passing, and wondered tentatively whether he should take Fong away from riot duty for the next few nights. He knew that the Sergeant would not crack, but he would be fast and heavy-handed with his riot stick for a while, and they could not afford any thin-skulled demonstrators left dead as Communist martyrs.

Chan had already explored the hold

and he looked up as Barratt joined him. The Superintendent knelt over the small body of the Chinese constable that sprawled face down, and noticed the large patch of red staining the bale beneath the dead man's left shoulder. He asked quietly:

"What was the cause of death?"

Chan's face was carved from yellow stone, and he pointed silently to a long-handled cargo hook with a dull-stained needle point that lay nearby.

"They killed him with that. Somebody reached from behind and hooked it into his throat."

3

The Price of Death

TWO hours passed before Barratt and Chan left the *Célérité* and their waiting car drove them back from Queen's Wharf to Eastern station. Barratt had taken statements from Tellier and his two officers, while Chan and the team of Chinese detectives who had followed them had thoroughly interrogated the Chinese crew. The mixture of reluctant and garbled statements from the seamen had added little to what Barratt had been told by Durdent. The argument in the hold had been the usual one, with agitators among the dock workers reviling the *Célérité*'s crewmen as traitors and lackeys of their French masters. There had been incitement to mutiny, and finally violence when one of the crew members had refused to acknowledge the divine thoughts of Chairman Mao Tse Tung.

The man who had attacked Constable Ho Kin from behind with the cargo hook had been described vaguely as one of the shore men; a Chinese perhaps thirty years old who had been wearing soiled blue overalls. The crew of the *Célérité* had all fled when they saw the constable fall, and then the murderer and his companions had quit the hold behind them and ran ashore. The dragnet that had been made of the wharf area as a whole had brought in a great many dockside workers, but they had all been adamant that it was strangers amongst them who had been the actual cause of the trouble, and that they had never before seen the man who had committed the murder. It had been vaguely suggested that the man might have been named Wong, but the name Wong was as frequent among the Chinese as the name Smith among the English. Barratt had a dozen Wongs as constables and two more as sergeants in his division alone, and the name, like the soiled blue overalls, could have belonged to any of a thousand hooligans let loose in the Colony.

The body of the dead man had been carried ashore and loaded into an ambulance, and Barratt had been in a black frame of mind as he watched it being driven off to the mortuary. Including the five men killed in the border raid at Sha Tau Kok the Colony's Police Force had now lost six of its Chinese constables, but this was the first man that Barratt had lost from his own division, and he knew that there was no real prospect of bringing the murderer to justice. Hong Kong was seething with resentment and unrest, and an investigation would only encounter closed mouths. In any event he would be kept too busy keeping down the riots and preventing more murders to make any concentrated attempt to solve this one. He was angered by the whole mess, and his temper had not been improved by Tellier who had begun to show an impatience to get his ship cleared of policemen so that the task of unloading her cargo could be continued.

Now, as the car weaved jerkily through the crowded streets, they sat in brooding silence until Chan opened his eyes and remarked quietly:

"Constable Ho Kin was married. He had a wife and two small babies. Would you prefer me to break the news to her?"

Barratt raised his head, hesitated frowning, and then nodded.

"It's my job, Charles, but it's also my job to take out the patrol tonight. So I'll be glad to accept your offer. I'll make a point of going round myself sometime tomorrow."

Chan closed his eyes again, a habit of his when he wished to think and not be distracted by the passing world with its flamboyant red-splashed shop signs and the bustle of life. The car jolted over tram lines as the driver swerved out to pass a slower taxi, and then Chan added in the same tone:

"The Constable should not have gone into that hold alone. That was a mistake."

Barratt was glad of an excuse to stop thinking of Ho Kin's unknowing widow and the two brand new orphans, and remembered the dead man himself, a slim, cheerful young man who had been still young enough to make mistakes. He said bluntly:

"He had more guts than muscle, and not enough experience."

"But it must not happen again. I will issue a definite order that no constable is to approach an argument or a mob alone. The order to be enforced while the emergency lasts."

Barratt nodded agreement. Already their men operated mostly in pairs, but if the general rule had been a standing order then Ho Kin might have stayed alive, and his family might have been spared their tears.

The car braked to a stop before

the old waterfront building that was Eastern police station and the two men got out. Barratt dismissed their driver and the car accelerated away. They turned and passed through the sandbag barrier to climb the steps to the open doorway. The sandbags and the loaded carbine of the young constable on sentry duty were recent additions to the station defences, and a constant reminder of the strong anti-British feelings running through the Colony. The sentry saluted and was briefly acknowledged.

They passed through the sliding, steel-meshed doors with Barratt in the lead. Inside a Chinese policewoman in a stiffly starched uniform was on duty at the telephone switchboard, and at the reception desk the duty sergeant was issuing orders to two young constables. As the two men turned away Barratt asked briefly:

"Anything to report?"

"On our side, no, sir." The Chinese sergeant straightened his shoulders briskly as he spoke. "Kowloon has had more trouble though, a massed riot with several men hurt by thrown bottles and stones. It was one of the worst yet, our men had to open fire and two of the demonstrators were killed."

"Blast!" Barratt exploded the word.

The sergeant hesitated uncertainly. "There were several thousand Chinese taking part in the demonstration, sir. The Kowloon police were almost swamped. The report says they had to open fire."

Barratt half turned and stared through the open doorway and across the street where the continuous traffic cut across his vision. Victoria's twin city of Kowloon was clearly visible across the intervening straits, a second, sprawling concrete jungle on the mainland of China. Now it was neon-lit with the first lights of evening, throwing a faint violet glow into the darkening velvet of the sky.

Barratt said grimly:

"So they've finally got their first

couple of martyrs. Blast again!"

Beside him Chan said bleakly:

"We can claim six martyrs. I think we have the lead."

The words seemed to act as a reminder of something to the man behind the desk. He said suddenly:

"Sergeant Weng Ki has come in, sir. He is waiting in the rest room. I think he has something to report."

"Then you'd better send him in."

Barratt turned away and marched down the whitewashed corridor to his office. Chan followed him inside. The Chinese Inspector took off his cap, hooked it on to the hat-stand, and automatically drew a comb from his breast pocket and passed it once through his black hair. As he watched the comb being returned Barratt reflected that he had never yet seen Chan with a hair out of place, or with a crumpled shirt. Chan was a model of smartness and efficiency for the rest of the station to copy.

Chan said matter-of-factly:

"If Kowloon has suffered this afternoon then we can expect a riot here tonight. The organizers on our side will not wish to appear to be lagging behind."

"We'll be prepared," Barratt said.

He poured two glasses from the large jug of iced lemon squash that was kept permanently on the table beside the large grey filing cabinet and handed one to Chan. The other he poured into his own dry throat. It was, he claimed, his only vice. He neither drank nor smoke, and even if he had not been contentedly married his job left him no time to chase women.

Chan drank more slowly. He rarely showed any signs of being affected by the heat. A knock sounded on the door behind him and he half-turned his head to answer. The door opened and a young Chinese in his mid-twenties came inside. He wore a grubby white sweat shirt, blue trousers and scuffed canvas shoes, but despite the shabby apparel he was fit and solid with sharply intelligent eyes. His clothes were a lie which he discarded now as he held his head back and saluted briskly. Barratt sat down behind the desk to receive him and found half a smile.

"Come in, Sergeant. What have you got this time?"

Weng Ki lowered his arm but did not fully relax as he approached the desk. He was part of the ghost squad of plain clothes detectives whom Barratt had mingling with the crowds in the streets, and now his face was more serious than usual.

"It's just a rumour, sir, but not a pleasant one."

"What kind of rumour?"

"The news is in the streets that one of our men was killed aboard a ship at Queen's Wharf. And the talk says that the man who killed him will be paid three-hundred sterling pounds. The Communists have put a bounty on the head of every policeman in Hong Kong."

Barratt pushed his glass to one side

46

and stared up at the Sergeant's face.

"Are you sure about this?"

"It is only talk, sir, but I think that it must be true."

"All right, what's the procedure for collecting the blood money? Does the talk tell that?"

Weng Ki blinked, the only movement of his flat, round face.

"No, sir. But the demonstrators and the riot-makers know which of those amongst them are the paid agitators. The agitators are the lowest link of the chain, and through them the money would probably be collected."

Barratt pulled a bitter expression on to his craggy face, as though his last sip of lemon squash had suddenly turned sour in his mouth. Then he asked:

"What else does the talk say? Are they planning anything for tonight?"

"I am not certain." Weng Ki was apologetic. "But I think there will be trouble. The news has spread about the rioting in Kowloon this afternoon, and they know that two demonstrators have been shot dead. It is all that the agitators need to urge the mobs into a fresh protest, which means another riot."

Barratt nodded in agreement. "Take care then, Sergeant. And take a meal and a break before you go back on the streets."

Weng Ki nodded, and recognizing his dismissal he turned and went out. Barratt turned his head to face Chan and said grimly:

"It's a bad sign. There will be a lot of men willing to earn those three-hundred pound bounties."

Chan sat down at his own desk, folded his hands across his blotter, and said calmly:

"It was to be expected. We already know that the Communists are paying in hard cash for most of the trouble they stir up. A day's work of rioting can earn a man forty Hong Kong dollars, and even the small boys get a dollar for every bucketful of throwing stones that they can collect." He smiled briefly. "Did you know that one little eight-year-old actually complained to one of our men because he was being underpaid by fifty cents."

The smile vanished as he concluded: "I am not surprised that the rates of pay now include a set fee for murder."

Barratt said wearily: "And we know how the money gets in — from Peking via the Bank of China and the offices of the *People's Daily* here in Hong Kong. And there's nothing we can do about it. The party bosses sit up there on the top floors of their skyscrapers, smug as hell, and knowing full well that as near as damnit they're enjoying diplomatic protection. We can't touch either of those buildings without pushing Mao into a positive retaliation."

Chan smiled sadly, with no humour touching his slit eyes.

"As you say, we cannot touch the shepherds, we can only hope to control the rampaging sheep. And when you consider the poverty that exists behind the façade of Hong Kong, in the shanty towns and the sampan jungles, it is difficult to blame them. Forty dollars simply for throwing stones and breaking windows is a large temptation for a man who would otherwise be breaking his back in a textile mill for perhaps as little as four to ten dollars. There is much here for the Communists to exploit."

Barratt nodded, and quite suddenly it occurred to him precisely why he held Chan in such high regard. Chan was not the usual kind of native colonial policeman who railed and cursed at his own people to show that he had changed sides, for Chan had not changed sides. Chan was Chinese, with sympathy and understanding for the problems of his fellows in this little corner of leased China, and within that framework he was the best kind of police officer that the Colony could have. The Communists had applied to him their standard label of 'imperialist tool', but in this case they had never been more wrong.

4

The 'Golden Mandarin'

THE island of Hong Kong like the neighbouring city of Kowloon across the straits was becoming alive with neon. From the summit of the Peak, where the yellow street lights along the climbing road on the lower slopes were like loops of stringed golden pearls, both cities were spread out in all their nightly glory. Each one was a vast maze of sparkling lights and great, whitely-illuminated blocks, cut by canyons of moving red and yellow fire that were the traffic-congested streets. The harbour between was like black silk, with red reflections like stains of blood from the crimson neon signs along the Kowloon waterfront. While the lights of the scattered ships at anchor were so numerous that in places it was impossible to tell where the land ended and the sea began. The nine hills of Kowloon and the New Territories beyond were already hidden in darkness.

At the foot of the Peak the narrow, steeply ascending ladder streets, that had been so busy during the day were now quiet. The little shops and market stalls where practically anything and everything could be found if you looked long enough were shuttered and closed for the night. In the lower arteries of Queens and Des Voeux Roads the traffic still bustled impatiently, but in the towering commercial buildings and office blocks, although they were still brightly lit, the day had also ended. The Star Ferry boats disgorged and absorbed their full quota of passengers every five minutes at the ferry pier beneath the impressive shadow of the City Hall, but now the main hub of life had moved definitely to the east. The night was young, but the girlie bar jungle of Wanchai had come into its own.

There were scores of bars, brash and garish with exotic names like *The Pussycat*, *The Keyhole*, *The Cave*, *The Manhattan*, *The Old Toby*, and a more recent addition, *The Suzie Wong*. Inside the bars sat the Suzie Wongs themselves, hundreds of them in their bare-armed, highnecked *cheongsens*, and each one casually displaying a bare slit of white thigh. They sat on the high-topped stools chatting to their customers at the bars, or sat and gossiped amongst themselves at the tables, or else simply smoked their cigarettes and hopefully watched the doors. In the crowded streets outside the rickshaw boys and the taxi drivers touted for custom, grinning the eternal promises of tarnished delight. The British and American sailors prowled cheerfully, ignoring the advice of their officers who had told them that beer was three times cheaper in the China Fleet Club, and that a night spent there didn't entail the embarrassment of standing in line for their penicillin shots in the morning.

The Golden Mandarin was one of the many bars, much like all the others with its brightly illuminated frontage and its prettiest hostess leaning idly in the half open doorway to smile at the passing sailors. The Golden Mandarin was portrayed in yellow neon on the prominent sign above her head, the head and shoulders of a smiling pantomime chinaman with long drooping moustaches, and taloned fingernails on the hands clasped sedately across his chest. Inside the bar was faced with studded yellow leather, and the high bar stools were all yellow-topped. Golden yellow was the featured colour of the decor, but the lights were dim except for those above the bar. Business was warming up, and the bar girls were laughing with, and calculating their prospective customers. While they laughed they sipped their way expertly through endless glasses of disguised fruit juice at cocktail prices.

In a room above the bar Lee Kung stood by the open window, staring down past the golden mandarin sign to the moving pattern of briefly yellow-lit faces that passed along the pavement below.

Lee Kung was displeased. He had expected to be taken direct to the Bank of China, or the office of the *People's Daily*, but instead he had been brought here to a down-town brothel. After the sewer crossing it was a double affront to his dignity. He heard the door behind him open and close, but did not turn immediately. He was entitled to respect, and would issue invitations in his own time.

The intruder did not wait to be invited. Lee Kung heard footsteps cross the patterned carpet, a slight rustling from a silk dress, and then the clink of a bottle against a glass. He turned angrily and recognized the black one, the one who had no respect. She was a small woman, hard and old, and her name was Madame Chong. She ran *The Golden Mandarin* and six other girlie bars, two more here in Wanchai, and a further four in downtown Kowloon on the opposite side of the straits. She wore a black dress, and her black hair was coiffured into a close modern style. Her bare arms were not yet skinny and her figure was still reasonably good, and it was only in the age lines of her face that her sixty years fully showed. She poured a cut glass tumbler one third full of whisky from a bottle of Black Label Johnny Walker, and asked calmly:

"Will you drink, Comrade Kung?"

Lee Kung said coldly. "It is a weakness to rot the stomach and the mind with strong drink, a decadent weakness that you have copied from the sailors and tourists who use your bars."

Madame Chong moved her shoulders impassionately and drank some of her whisky neat. She watched him with detached hatred in her slitted eyes, and if he had not known that her hatred embraced all men Lee Kung might have found it disconcerting. However, he knew that her hatred was controlled, it was a suppressed thing that had only served to embitter her heart and soul, and offered no outward danger. Madame Chong had a sharp business head that far outweighed any emotion. As if she had not heard his condemnation of her weakness she said in the same flat tone as before:

"They will arrive at eight o'clock, one representative from each section of the party."

Lee Kung scowled. "It would have been better if the meeting was to be held at the Bank of China, or in the building of the *People's Daily*, or even at the headquarters of any one of the trade unions. Why must it be held here?"

The old woman drank more whisky and then answered:

"Because all of those places that

you have named are being constantly watched by spies of the British police. This does not prevent us from using most of these places for the purposes of routine organization, of which the police involving a gathering of high-placed party officials who would be easily recognized then this is a better place. *The Golden Mandarin* is one centre on which the police are not yet informed. The meeting has more privacy."

"Yet it has less safety. The police can find a legitimate excuse to raid a brothel, while they would not dare to enter either the bank or the press building. Have you considered that?"

"Everything is considered, Comrade Kung." Her face was as expressionless as cold parchment. "That is why the police have no cause to suspect this place, which in turn is why it will be safe. Even in normal times the police do not make blind raids upon the bars without reason, and tonight they will be too busy controlling the streets."

Lee Kung could find no solid argument, and turned his back on her to stare out through the window. Madame Chong drained the rest of her whisky without blinking, set down the glass and moved towards the door. She paused there and said:

"There is an hour to wait — shall I send you a girl?"

Lee Kung turned, restraining his temper, and said harshly:

"No, Comrade Chong, I do not want a girl."

The old woman nodded, as though his desires were of no importance, and then went out. Lee Kung glared at the door as she closed it behind her, and he could feel frustration gnawing in his loins. He did want a girl, but having spoken out against her weakness he would lose face by indulging his own. His glance fell upon the empty tumbler and the whisky bottle which she had left standing openly on the low table as though to tempt him, and he had to check the impulse to walk across

59

and send them both crashing with a sweep of his hand. That would be childish and would also lose him face. He turned away again and began to glare once more through the window.

* * *

The meeting assembled at eight o'clock precisely, and was held in another large room above *The Golden Mandarin*. It was a room normally reserved for private parties, but now the soft chairs, drapes and furnishings had been cleared away to give a more austere appearance fitting to the present occasion. The large screen and the blue film projector had been removed, and now the room held a large polished table, bare even of ashtrays, and a dozen surrounding, stiff-backed chairs. Twelve persons were gathered, including Lee Kung and Madame Chong. There were four trade union leaders who had journeyed across the straits from Kowloon, two from unions resident here in Hong Kong, and two representative officials from each of the main sources of Communist leadership, the high citadels of the *People's Daily* and the Bank of China. Madame Chong was the only woman present.

The introductions were made and Lee Kung attempted to weigh up each man as his name was revealed in turn. They were a ring of polished yellow faces, as readable as the brown oak of the table-top before them. Only the slitted eyes revealed anything, either distrust or anger as they met his gaze. All of them wore conventional western suits and none of them outwardly showed any fear. Lee Kung was certain of only one thing, there were no weak men here. All of them were high-level party members, dedicated and uncompromising. Yet they had failed, and he had to prove himself stronger than them all.

Madame Chong named the last man, one of the two finance experts from the Bank of China. He made the final slow nod of acknowledgement, and the first fractional relaxing of the facial muscles which might have been a still-born smile. The money channelled from Peking passed through and was controlled by his hands, and he knew that in his field at least there was no fault. The money had not been lacking, and it was amongst his fellows that any blame must fall.

The tall party man from Canton stood upright, the table fell silent, and he delivered his prepared tongue-lashing with no time-wasting preludes.

"Comrades, you know why you are here. You know why I am here. All of you received clear directives from party headquarters in Peking explaining exactly what you were to achieve. The total disruption of Hong Kong ... The humiliation of the imperialist governors of Hong Kong ... An endorsement from the British Government acknowledging the rightful sovereignty of the People's Republic of China over Hong Kong ... An agreement that Hong Kong must cease to be a military base for the imperialists, and that Hong Kong must cease to shelter the American murderers from Vietnam . . . And finally an agreement that all political prisoners must be released, and that all enemies of China who have fled to Hong Kong must be returned to face trial in the People's Republic. All this you were to have achieved by first creating a situation in which the British Government would have no choice but to accept our demands. Yet you have failed. Despite explicit instructions, three months of time, and unlimited funds, *you have all failed!*"

Lee Kung paused grimly in his tirade but there was no interruption. The ten men and the one woman sitting around the table all knew that he had not finished yet. They sat stiffly, and in frigid silence. Lee Kung looked around the circle, and then continued:

"In Canton the wall posters demand that you should all be brought back to confess your failure, and in Peking there is also much impatience. But a vast amount of money has already been spent on this simple project which you have failed to achieve, and so you are granted an extra space of time in which to redeem yourselves. Unlimited funds will continue to be available for the next two weeks. If you fail again there will be no more reprieve. You will all be recalled to Peking."

There was another moment of silence, then uncertainty as those around the table looked warily for another to speak. One of the two men from the *People's Daily* cleared his throat and then said frankly:

"Perhaps success is not possible, and we cannot perform miracles."

"Your comrades in Macao were successful," Lee Kong snapped back. "And there is no excuse for not carrying out the instructions of the party."

"The British are not the Portuguese,"

64

the same man said more harshly. "They cannot be panicked into opening fire as the Portuguese were in Macao. While the British keep their heads we cannot create the necessary situation where they would have to submit to the demands from Peking."

"Then the British police forces *must* be panicked," Lee Kung emphasized tartly.

One of the union men, a younger man seated on the opposite side of the table leaned forward abruptly, almost eagerly.

"The British were panicked, Comrade. Today in Kowloon. During the protest demonstration which I helped to organize they shot dead two Chinese. Is not this what we want? There will be fresh protests tomorrow when we shall demand that the British admit their responsibility for these two brutal murders. We shall demand that they pay compensation to the families of the dead men, and that they punish the murderers."

"It is not enough." Lee Kung crushed the speaker with his cold voice. "This afternoon the British lost five of their constables killed at Sha Tau Kok. The world counts the statistics of death. We will claim police brutality, but while there are more dead policemen than demonstrators we are not in the best position. If the police had killed a score of demonstrators, or even a dozen, then that would be good."

He slapped the palm of his hand hard upon the table and added. "If there were sufficient violence in your demonstrations then the British would have to meet them with more violence. They would have to kill more demonstrators to defend themselves. Why is there not sufficient violence? You have all the money you need, and there are thousands of Chinese to take part in your demonstrations."

It was the man from the *People's Daily* who answered:

"The reason, Comrade Kung, is

because many of the people of Hong Kong are not truly with us. They take their wages and play their parts, but they will not give their lives for the revolution. Many of the old ones came from China, and do not wish to return, or be returned. It is only with the young men that we are fully successful, the youths who were born here and know only their present grievances. They have no bad memories of China."

Lee Kung tightened his lips and his palm struck the table a second time in anger.

"There are no bad memories. There is no such thing. Do you dare to criticize the People's Republic of China? Do you dare to criticize the party?"

The words were a shout and the man from the *People's Daily* closed his mouth tight until he paled about the lips. He knew that he had made a bad mistake, and self-preservation kept him silent.

Madame Chong broke the hostile atmosphere, speaking for the first time. Her voice was hoarsely calm as always:

"Comrade Kung, we have already taken steps to panic the British police forces as you desire. Today one of their Chinese constables was killed in the docks. He will be only the first, and I have allowed the fact that three hundred pounds in English money was paid to purchase his death to circulate in the streets. Soon more will be killed, and every policeman in Hong Kong will know that his uniform makes him a marked man. Then they will panic, with thoughts of vengeance in their minds and fears for their own lives they will start to kill demonstrators. I have made plans also for their English officers, and for the senior administrators of the Colony. When the Chinese constables see that their masters cannot protect themselves, then they will break. The two weeks that you have given us will be sufficient time."

Lee Kung towards her, his eyes like slits of black ice.

"For your sake I will pray that you are right, for *all* your sakes. And now explain to me in more detail what you have planned."

5

Bad Girl

IN another of the many rooms above *The Golden Mandarin* Jenny Peng was entertaining an American sailor in the traditional manner, fully unaware of the portentous gathering that was taking place close by. Jenny was nineteen years old, dark haired, and still retained her youthful Chinese beauty. She was the youngest of the bar girls and a favourite attraction among the customers. At the moment her shoes stood neatly together at the foot of the bed, and her red *cheongsen* was laid just as neatly over the chair beside the small table on which stood two glasses and the full bottle of whisky that she had persuaded the sailor to buy and bring up to her room. It was now part of her job to ensure that he did not drink too much so that a profitable percentage could be returned to the bar. However, she was performing her task only absently, and was hardly aware of the weight and the thrusting movement of the man pressing her slim body down on to the bed, for tonight Jenny Peng was deeply troubled in mind.

She had been born in China in a small village near the great industrial city of Changsha on the Siang River. When she was one year old the Communist armies had marched southward from Manchuria to attack the Kuomintang government of the Nationalists and drive them out to Taiwan, and although she had then been too young to understand she had witnessed the greater and far bloodier birth of the new People's Republic. Her father had been a small merchant, and a supporter of Chiang Kai-Shek, and somehow he had escaped the initial purges by the triumphant Communists. Five years later, when the child was old enough to remember more clearly, his past had come to light in a new purge. Jenny could remember the shouting men who had come to take her father away, and the wailing of her mother, and the crushing arms of her mother's sister who had held her close and prevented her from following her father outside. Her aunt had told her much later that the Communists had tied her father's hands behind his back, and then cut off his head with a sword in his own backyard. It had been a routine execution.

The child's mother had died soon afterwards. They had been forced to leave the house where they had lived with her father and move to a small hovel. There the mother had coughed out her life in a starved fever. The aunt had taken care of Jenny Peng, who was not named Jenny then, but she too had lost a husband in the purges and was reviled as a Nationalist's widow. Their home was no longer a home, and like many others before her the old woman had bundled up what few possessions she could carry, and taking the child by the hand had started to walk south. She had heard that Chiang Kai-Shek and his government had taken refuge on an island called Taiwan, and that there was a place called Hong Kong which was part of China but where the Communists did not rule. She only knew that both places were somewhere to the south of Changsha.

Jenny Peng was seven when she and her old aunt had crossed the border into the New Territories of the Crown Colony of Hong Kong, just two of the seemingly endless streams of refugees from the Communist mainland. The old aunt had found a job working the treadmill of a loom in a basement factory ten hours a day for a few shillings a week, and had considered herself very fortunate. The few shillings bought food, and she and the child were allowed to sleep in a bare corner. Two years later the child was allowed to work the next loom.

Their fortunes changed for the

better after three years when the aunt successfully married another worker named Lui Yeung whose first wife had died and left him with three children of varying ages. Lui Yeung owned a dilapidated sampan aboard which he lived with his family, and the duties of a wife and mother to three additional orphans had seemed a reasonable exchange for escape from the loom and a home aboard the sampan. All the parties concerned were satisfied, including Jenny Peng, for although she still had to work daily at her loom she now had two four-foot lengths of the sampan's deckboards to call her own at night.

For a further five long and weary years Jenny Peng toiled at her loom, hidden from the eyes of the world in the dreary basement factory, and then good fortune smiled upon her in turn. She had developed into a very pretty seventeen-year-old, with pert breasts and shapely hips that showed through her shabby cotton working suit, and

a few dollars each week. She hoped that when she had saved up enough dollars as a dowry she might be able to find a respectable young man like the factory manager's younger son who would marry her. She knew that it was possible, because other girls had saved up and made respectable marriages even after being a bar girl. And with no false modesty she knew that she was prettier than all the other girls in *The Golden Mandarin*, and in most of the other bars around.

However, even with the happy ending visible in her dreams it seemed that fate intended to be unkind to her. With great misgivings she had watched the massed riots and the voilent upheavals that had racked the whole of Hong Kong during the preceding weeks, and with no comprehension of the propaganda and political issues at stake she feared that the Communists intended nothing less than to take over the whole Colony.

Jenny Peng did not want that to

happen. She remembered Communist China as a black and terrible land where she had always been cold and hungry, where her clothes had always been rags and her blistered and bleeding feet had walked over endless rough and stony miles. She also remembered Communist China as the place where they had cut off her father's head with a sword, and then forced her mother to leave their nice home and die in a dark hut. Some of her friends who had never been there, the ones who went to the political meetings and recited the thoughts of Chairman Mao Tse Tung, told her that all was different now, and that Red China was a wonderful place. But Jenny Peng did not believe them. She believed her memories, and she did not want Hong Kong to become like the place of her memories.

Jenny Peng wanted Hong Kong to remain exactly as it was, a British territory where the British and American sailors could come in never-ending numbers to laugh and drink and freely spend their money; and where an ordinary bar girl could save up and hope to get married.

Now she was very much afraid that all this would come to an end, and that the Communists would take over Hong Kong and that there would be nowhere else for her to go. If there had been nothing that she could do then she would have resigned herself to whatever the fates might decide, and stoically accept any new pains and sufferings that she might have to bear, but this time there was something that she could do. It was perhaps a very little thing this thing of which she knew, but perhaps it would help the British authorities against the Communists if she could find the way and the courage to approach them. This was the root cause of her worried mind, the fact that perhaps she could help fight the Communists if only she could tell the right person of the thing of which she knew. Her aunt and her new uncle would not know how to advise her, and there was no one else whom she could really trust, and she was very confused, uncertain and afraid.

★ ★ ★

She became suddenly aware that the sailor above her had finished. His body had become still and was heavy upon her. She blinked and focused her eyes, realizing that he was looking down at her with an expression of puzzled disappointment at her lack of response. He said almost angrily:

"Say, Jenny Honey, you weren't even with me."

Jenny Peng smiled quickly, pushing her thoughts away because she wanted the sailor to come back to her again. He was not ungenerous and he did not ask her to do the unusual things that she did not want to do. She coiled her nude arms and legs around him and squeezed him tightly, almost with affection.

"You are very good lover-boy," she

assured him. "You make me close my eyes, and dream beautiful dreams of pleasure."

She smiled again and repeated: "Yes, you are very good lover!"

6

Daughter of the Horse

MADAME CHONG returned to her private apartment after the meeting had disbanded with a definite feeling of relief. She did not fear Lee Kung but she disliked him intensely, just as she disliked all men. She needed to be alone in her apartment where no man had ever been permitted to enter. She broke the seal on a new bottle of Black Label Johnny Walker, and poured herself a large tumblerful of neat whisky. She drank and let the spirit burn the sour taste of the meeting from her mouth. She did not want to think about the meeting, or the men who had taken part. To her they were all fools.

Her apartment consisted of two private rooms and a bathroom on the top floor above *The Golden Mandarin*. One room was a lavishly furnished office where she kept her business accounts and private papers, together with a small steel safe. A personal maid was allowed to clean here and in the bathroom, but no one at all was allowed into the bedroom where she now stood. No one but herself had ever slept on the large canopied bed with its blue silk drapes, and no other feet but her own had walked across the deep, blue-piled carpet that covered the floor. The room also contained a large dressing-table, carved from teak in oriental design. There was an elaborate Japanese screen across the door, and Japanese prints were framed and hung against the grey-pastel walls. There was a final link with Japan that also hung upon one wall, the heavy blade of a sheathed samurai sword.

Madame Chong gazed reflectively at the sword as she drank her whisky, and wondered again why she had hung it there with the fading prints of Fujiyama, the sacred mountain, and the golden pavilion in the gardens of Kyoto, to remind her of the land that she hated almost as much as she hated men. Somewhere inside her there was an unknown something that still demanded some small link with her birthplace, despite all the cold brutality of her logical mind. For although Madame Chong had posed as Chinese for many years, she had been born in Nagoya on the main island of Honshu in Japan.

At her birth Madame Chong had been named Asami Hinata, and she had been born in the year of Hinoeuma, the dreaded year of the Fire and the Horse. It was the worst possible year for a girl child to be born, for according to an old Japanese superstition a girl born during this year was liable to murder any husband she might later acquire. The year of Hinoeuma occurred in the Japanese calendar only once every sixty years, and even during enlightened nineteen-sixty-six when the year had come again there had been a sharp drop in the Japanese birth rate. There had also been a sharp rise in abortions, for even modern Japanese couples remembered the old superstitions and preferred to bear no child at all rather than risk giving birth to a girl.

In the year of nineteen-o-six, the previous year of Hinoeuma, there had been no modern methods of birth control, and no easy methods of abortion, and so many girl children like Asami Hinata had had the great misfortune to be born. Tainted by the year of her birth, and for ever a daughter of the horse, there had been no possibility that such a girl would ever find a husband, or lead a normal married life. The fears of the old superstition caused them to be shunned and rejected.

So it was not surprising that after puberty Asami Hinata developed an increasing hatred for fate, for life, and most especially for all men. Her childhood had been very happy, and perhaps her parents had tried very hard in those early years to compensate her for the later disillusionment and sufferings of womanhood. They had explained the nature of her blight when she was fourteen, when the first sexual awakenings had begun within her, and when the young men with whom she had been childhood friends had been warned by their parents to avoid her. Those early sexual desires were never naturally relieved, for by the time she had decided to break from Japan and leave its superstitions behind her hatred had hardened towards those who had spurned her, and she no longer wanted to be touched by any man.

It was in nineteen twenty-nine that the parents of Asami Hinata died, leaving her their middle-class home in Nagoya and their modest fortune. The embittered young woman was an only child, and with no ties she had sold up everything that her parents had left behind, and then booked her passage on a small steamer to Shanghai and a new life. She shed not a single tear and did not look back once to Japan as the steamer left Yokohama harbour, and she had never returned. China would not be her home, but at least it was the land where she expected to live out the rest of her life.

Alone in the strange new city of Shanghai she had quickly realized that she could rely only upon her own resources, and that if she was to survive then her money must be invested so that it could work for her and keep her alive. There were many difficulties, but she had arrived at a turbulent phase of China's history, a time of change when fate toppled emperors, made generals out of peasants, caused the deaths of thousands, and made fortunes for the few. She had been able to buy the premises of a cheap, waterfront bar from a less hard-headed widow whose husband had been knifed to death in a brawl, and with a natural head for business she had quickly combined the bar with the functions of a brothel. Sometimes in those early days she had catered for the needs of some of her customers herself, but she entertained only the sorrier kind of men with a whip and never with her body. It pleased her to see the hated creatures crawl and make fools of themselves. She felt that they owed her a lifetime of revenge. She had come to Shanghai with a smattering of mandarin Chinese, and had set herself the task of mastering the language. She took the Chinese name of Chong, and because of her trade she was called Madame. Madame Chong was born, and the luckless Asami Hinata, unwept and unmourned, was dead and buried forever.

In nineteen-thirty-one the Japanese in their efforts to expand their empire had invaded Manchurian China, and within six years the whole of the country was ravaged by general warfare. They were dark and bloody times, and it was as well for Madame Chong that she had buried her Japanese identity. Then came nineteen-forty-one, and the great city and seaport of Shanghai was itself occupied by the conquering Japanese troops. The waterfront bar owned by Madame Chong became a favourite rendezvous for Japanese soldiers, where they both drank and talked freely.

Madame Chong despised the swaggering invaders, and the hatred that burned so much more fiercely for the men of her own homeland, together with an acute business eye to the future, had caused her to play a dangerous game. Like a Chinese Mata Hari she had taken careful note of every fragment of military information that she had overheard, and then passed them on to one of the Chinese undercover agents working in the city. She did not know how her offerings were passed out of the city to the south, or whether they ever served any real purpose, but they were to have an important bearing on later events. So was the fact that by pure chance she had passed those reports through an agent of one of the

Communist administrations rather than an agent of the then crumbling National government of the Kuomintang.

Japan's dreams of an empire had died in the nuclear ashes of Nagasaki and Hiroshima at the end of the second world war, and the Japanese troops had departed from the soil of China. More internal strife followed before the future of China was finally settled by the Communist armies expelling Chiang Kai-Shek and his Nationalist followers, but throughout this period Madame Chong had restricted her activities to the running of her Shanghai bar. The Japanese had been a special case and she had strongly desired their defeat, but in the civil wars that followed she cared little or nothing who won or lost in divided China.

It was not until the Communists had achieved complete control and united the vast Asian land mass under the iron chairmanship of Mao Tse Tung that Madame Chong had experienced any direct dealings with the Communist party. Then, after a few years she had been approached by a deputation of three serious-faced party officials. The fact that she had passed information during the Japanese occupation of Shanghai still existed somewhere in their records, and now they placed a new proposition before her. She was offered sufficient funds to set herself up with a new and far more expensive and elaborate brothel and bar on the British Crown Colony of Hong Kong. In return she was to again collect from the girls she employed any items of information that could be gleaned from the British and American sailors who thronged the port.

Madame Chong possessed no politics whatsoever, she was alone and served no one but herself. However, as a solid business proposition she had considered the offer and then accepted it. In nineteen-fifty-three she had come from Shanghai to Hong Kong, and financed by the Communists she had opened *The Scarlet Dragon* in Kowloon.

Over the next thirteen years she had gradually built up her brothel empire, partly through her own natural flair for business, and partly with the aid of Communist funds. She now controlled a total of seven girlie bars, and the latest, the biggest and the best was *The Golden Mandarin* here in Wanchai.

She had not bargained for the present state of affairs in Hong Kong, and in fact had little liking for them. They caused too much disruption to her trade. However, her paymasters were rigid totalitarians, and because she knew that they could destroy her if she failed them Madame Chong had worked as hard as any in the organization of the troubles. For her own protection she had to work to achieve all Communist aims, and her lack of any true political feeling had been made irrelevant. Even before the arrival of Lee Kung she had faced the possibility that she might be called to Canton or Peking with the others to confess her part in the general failure to humiliate the stubborn British, and so she had set her mind and her energies to ensuring that the aims of Peking were realized.

The thought of Lee Kung brought the sour taste back to her mouth, and she took another large sip at her whisky. The tumbler was nearly empty and she turned away from the long samurai sword upon the wall and set the tumbler down upon the small side cabinet that contained the bottle and glasses. She knew that tonight she had drunk too much of the neat spirit, and she could not afford an unclear head that might make mistakes. There was a tense feeling inside her that made her cross to the table by her bedside and pull open the lower drawer. The whip lay like a coiled snake of black leather, thickening into the short stock. It was a long time since she had indulged in using the whip, and she knew that she craved the pleasure of thrashing Lee Kung. It was a dangerous thought, and one that she knew she could never practise. The scotch whisky was taking hold of her head.

She slammed the drawer shut and then went to use the bathroom. She had made up her mind that she would not leave her rooms again that night. She was obliged to have Lee Kung on her premises, but at least she could avoid him.

7

Riot Patrol

JACK BARRATT sat in the front seat of the crawling police Land Rover and watched the crowded pavements of Wanchai moving slowly past. He wore a steel helmet in place of his peaked cap, which meant that in effect he had ceased to be a Divisional Superintendent and was now the troop commander of a riot platoon. He always felt that he had made a transfer from the police force to the army whenever he was obliged to don his steel hat. Behind him sat a small mobile squad of six helmeted Chinese constables and one sergeant, all armed with carbines and tear gas guns, and with wickerwork shields to protect them from thrown missiles if they became necessary. So far it had been a relatively quiet night, and they had broken up only three gangs of roving hooligans and made only two arrests, which meant that the mass demonstration he had anticipated had probably been deferred until tomorrow.

The Land Rover's two-way radio crackled constantly as they listened in to the string of reports passing between Eastern station, and the other three mobiles that made up tonight's patrol, and from time to time Barratt flipped the switch on his mike to report their own position. He had left Chan in charge of the station, preferring to get out into the streets as often as possible to keep his finger on the city's pulse, and it sounded as though Chan was having the usually busy time as the four mobiles fed him a stream of suspected criminals and political agitators. The four police divisions in Hong Kong undertook riot duty in nightly rotation, and tonight the whole of Eastern was on alert.

The bars, the brothels and the dance

halls were doing their usual lively trade, and the massed neon signs overhanging the streets joined with the perpendicular shop signs with their strange oriental characters in a firm effort to shut out the higher darkness of the night sky. The pavements were filled with babble and movement, and a racial mixture of faces that emerged from shadow into the glow of the lights and then vanished into shadow again. Some of the faces were American, topped by U.S. Navy caps, some were British, and the vast majority were the flat moon faces of the Chinese, all of them flickering through the changing colours of the lights and darkness.

The traffic was heavy, and American taxies, a big red bus, overloaded and swaying, and faster private cars all swished past the idling Land Rover, adding to the noise and confusion. There was the smell of exhausts mixed with the fainter smells of noodles and steaming food pans from a Chinese soup kitchen. Somewhere mah jong chips clipped and rattled to indicate a group of Chinese gamblers at an unseen table, and from behind the half closed doors and curtains of the bars came the clink of glasses, uncaring voices and rowdy laughter.

Barratt was carefully scrutinizing the sea of passing faces, looking for the first scowling signs of trouble. They passed a wrinkled old Chinaman who had drawn his red-painted rickshaw close against the curb and was talking volubly to a pair of obviously English tourists. The man was smiling through gapped teeth and gesturing emphatically with his hands, and Barratt knew that he was touting for some hidden vice hole. However, tonight Barratt was not interested in collecting touts. The Land Rover passed on, and then the sergeant in the back pointed over Barratt's shoulder to indicate a slim young Chinese who was walking much more slowly than the main crowds and allowing the swirl of bodies to brush against him. Barratt recognized a known pickpocket, but the man became aware of his danger with some strange, criminal instinct, and turned abruptly to vanish into a bar. Barratt decided that tonight he would ignore pickpockets too, and refrained from sending a pair of his constables in chase. With patience they would almost certainly catch the man red-handed the next time there was a race meeting at Happy Valley.

Further along three drunken American sailors reeled noisily about the pavement. The Land Rover stopped, but Barratt had already seen the two-man shore patrol of burly American MPs cutting through the crowds towards the unsteady trio. He watched for a moment until he was satisfied that no assistance was needed, and then he nodded for his driver to carry on.

The Land Rover turned a corner where a small group of Chinese had gathered. The talk stopped as the Land Rover appeared, but the men held their ground and stared back sullenly at Barratt and the constables inside. Again the driver turned an enquiring glance, but after a fractional hesitation Barratt again shook his head. The group consisted of older men and was not quite large enough to warrant a forced dispersal. Barratt knew that he was faced with the seemingly impossible task of playing his job both hard and soft at one and the same time. Hong Kong had to be kept under tight police control, and yet he could not afford to give the Communists any grounds for their continuous cries of 'Provocation' The only solution was to cruise soft, but to strike hard when it became necessary. Tonight, with the Gurkhas still facing the Red Chinese frontier guards in a dubious armed truce over machine-guns at Sha Tau Kok, he was hoping that he could get away with cruising soft. The main shock waves from this afternoon's violence in Kowloon had clearly been delayed in crossing the straits, and he had hopes that the quiet night would continue.

The Land Rover turned another corner on to Gloucester Road which ran along the waterfront, and picked up speed a little as they drove east. There were fewer crowds here, but Barratt gave the order to keep going. They left the bar jungle behind and Barratt gave another order to douse the headlights as they drew up before the typhoon anchorage at the end of the road. Here he got out to stretch his legs, watching and listening. The work of unloading was going on aboard one or two of the big sea-going junks close by, the dock labourers busily carrying large bales upon their backs as they stepped back and forth across the narrow planks that spanned between the decks and the quay. There was a little noise, some banging, panting and shouting, but beyond all was quiet. The lights twinkled from the mass of small sampans cluttering the back end of the anchorage, casting faint, shining patterns over the black water. Somewhere in that floating world of poverty a child was probably being born; an old man was probably dying; and a great number of young couples would be making hopeless love while their closely-crowded families pretended not to watch or listen. It was an endlessly repeated pattern wherever the sampans were jumbled together, which was wherever there was room.

Barratt lingered only for a moment, and then climbed back into the Land Rover again. There was no scent of trouble here, and he did not want to be long away from the more likely breeding grounds. He made a brief radio report to Eastern while the police driver switched on his lights and reversed the Land Rover, then they were speeding back they way they had come.

The Land Rover took a left turn, away from the waterfront, and then swung right along the main Hennessy Road. They were back among the crowds and the traffic, and returning into the garish domain of the Suzie Wongs, and once more their speed slowed to a watchful crawl. Barratt was studying the streams of faces again, and then he saw one that was familiar. He gave a sharp order and the Land Rover braked to a stop.

Two of the constables tumbled swiftly out of the back. They ran towards a husky young Chinese in a soiled sweat shirt who had started to run away along the pavement and grabbed him as he tried to wriggle through the crowds. The Chinese protested in angry tones as they hustled him back to the waiting Land Rover. He was pushed roughly forward to lean with his hands pressed flat against the vehicle's steel sides just behind the cab, and one of the constables patted him over in a deft search for weapons. There were some angry mutterings from the pavement, and two more of the constables got down from the back of the van to make a show of force, their carbines held loosely.

Barratt did not look round, but spoke in a low voice:

"Anything to report, Sergeant?"

Sergeant Weng Ki smiled briefly, but in his undignified position with his arms braced forward and his head hanging down the smile was hidden against his chest. He did not look up as he answered in the same tone:

"Wanchai seems quiet, but the trouble will come tomorrow. I have trailed a man who was carrying a home-made bomb. He was trying to persuade a youth to take it into City Hall. He was very amateur and I kept both of them in sight until another of our mobiles came along. They made the arrest and took both men to the station to be charged. I have nothing now."

Barratt was never afraid to pay a compliment to a man doing a dangerous job. He said softly:

"Fine work, Sergeant. Keep it up."

He nodded briefly to the two constables and Weng Ki was pulled

104

away from the Land Rover and told curtly that he could go. The young sergeant answered loudly with a protest and an insult and was given a hard shove on to the pavement to help him on his way. He spat defiantly into the gutter and then melted quickly into the watching crowd. The constables climbed back into the Land Rover, ignoring the jeers that came when it began to move away. Once they were clear Barratt allowed himself a brief smile.

They turned left towards Wanchai Road, and Barratt pressed the switch on his hand mike to relay Weng Ki's report that the area was quiet. It was acknowledged and he switched back to receive. However, Weng Ki was not infallible, for five minutes later they overheard an urgent call for mobile three to break up a mob forming in Leighton Road. Barratt pressed the mike switch again.

"Mobile one to control, we'll cut in on that. We're reasonably close."

Without waiting for an acknowledgment the Chinese driver grinned and accelerated the Land Rover. He made a fast left turn as he swung into Wanchai Road itself, causing half a dozen startled Chinese to curse and scatter backwards from the pavement corner. Then his foot pressed hard down. Behind him the bored sergeant and his six constables had also begun to smile.

The disturbance was at the further end of Leighton Road and it took them just under ten minutes to reach the scene. Mobile three, an identical Land Rover with an eight man squad, including the sergeant in charge, had already arrived. The sergeant and six of his men had already scrambled down on to the road as mobile one braked to a stop, and Barratt's men ran to swell the small force. Beyond then a mob of over a hundred youths were running wild. Two private cars had already been toppled over and one was a blaze of fire. A third was being rocked back and forth by the hard core of the mob, and even as Barratt swung down from his cab the car tipped over with a resounding crash and the showering of broken glass. The mob howled in one voice, and then began to scatter before the advancing police. It was a scene that Barratt had witnessed a score of times during the present emergency, and this time he was relieved that he had only a minor pack of youths to deal with instead of one of the thousand-strong organized demonstrations.

Methodically, and with the confidence born of repeated practise the thirteen men of the combined riot squads spread out across the road with Barratt at their head and made a brisk baton charge into the crowd. The two Land Rovers followed up close behind, and Barratt's driver managed two jobs at once as he handled the wheel and at the same time passed a report on the situation through the hand mike gripped in his free hand. The mob jeered and hurled insults and stones in a retreating fight, and the air was filled with their taunting cries and the crash of more breaking glass as shop windows disintegrated in the general mêlée. Some of the fleeing youths attempted to double back past the line of stolid constables, and the line became disorganized as scuffles broke out at each end. Two of the more militant rioters yelled at their companions to stop and fight, and Barratt pin-pointed them immediately.

"Sergeant, arrest those two!"

The sergeant from mobile three and one of his constables rushed for the two ringleaders. Both youths ran but the constable chased and caught the smaller with a low baton-swipe across the side of the knee. The youth yelled and went down with his legs practically cut from under him, and then the constable had him by the collar. The second youth was a wilder young animal, despite the fact that he wore studious glasses. He ducked the rushing sergeant and butted him hard in the stomach. As the sergeant fell away gasping he turned to run, but Barratt himself sprinted forward to head him off. They met close by the blazing car and Barratt could feel the waves of heat searing his face as he dragged the youth to a stop. The youth screamed and struggled violently, and Barratt had to hit him once in the belly. The one blow was enough and he was able to drag the youth away from the fire and hand him over to another of the constables.

All was confusion now. Both Land Rovers had stopped and the combined riot squads were busy trying to hang on to the first of the mob leaders that they had captured. The two whom Barratt had pin-pointed had already been bundled into the back of mobile one but there were many others. The burning car crackled furiously and somewhere another window went, and then a hail of stones and other missiles began to rattle around their heads. A large chunk of masonry crashed noisily against the steel flank of mobile three, and a smaller stone gave Barratt a painful crack on the elbow. To his left he saw one of the constables stagger and almost fall as a lump of thrown wood cracked open the skin along his cheekbone. The rioters who had been in the forefront of the battle began to break away, running swiftly to join up with the stone-throwers who were fighting from a distance. Barratt spotted his sergeant with a tear gas gun and nodded grimly.

"Give them a taste, Sergeant. They've asked for it."

The sergeant smiled briefly, pulled his goggles down over his eyes, and then raised the short rifle to his shoulder and fired. The tear gas shell arced into the mob and smashed amongst them, and desperately they began to scatter again. Two more armed constables ran up and two more shells were fired. The stinging, acrid smell of the gas began to fill the streets and Barratt pulled down his own goggles to protect his eyes. All of his men followed his example. Where the gas was thickest the rioters were already coughing and reeling away with tears streaming down their cheeks. Some of them had to run back towards the waiting constables, and were given a sharp whack with a baton to help them on their way. Barratt and his men already had as many prisoners as they could handle, and the smaller fry were allowed to get away.

The mob was now definitely broken, despite the youths who still hurled stones and insults from a safe distance, and Barratt went back to mobile one to make his radio report, and to ask Chan to send out a van to collect the night's catch. As he handed the mike back to the constable at the wheel a new scuffle and a stream of curses broke out from the back of the Land Rover. Barratt moved round quickly and was just in time to help the constable standing guard to push back the young mob leader with the spectacles who had tried to break free.

The youth had recovered from the earlier blow in the stomach, but he remembered it and fell back with a curse as he recognized Barratt. He sucked in his cheeks as though he was about to spit, and then changed his mind as the constable threateningly lifted his carbine. Instead he turned his defiance into words:

"You are a fascist beast! One day you will pay for your brutality to the Chinese peoples!"

For a moment Barratt stared at him without answering. The flames from the distant fire cast a dull red glitter on to the youth's spectacles, and together with the snarling face gave him an almost demon look. Yet the youth could not have been more than nineteen or twenty years old, and like most of his comrades was probably a student. He had been born into an overcrowded rat race where thousands of children were born every year, and where most of his kind had no future but to toil out their lives in the sweat shops of the fat Chinese merchants. He knew of no other existence but his own and had good cause for rebellion. His home was most probably a sampan, or a shanty-town dog kennel hut on a hillside or a building block roof. His basic diet was almost certainly rice, with perhaps fish and occasional vegetables, and the white shirt on his back was possibly the only decent one he had. His family probably starved themselves to pay for his studies, and although he knew poverty he could look up to the rich, luxurious mansions that were reserved for the five-per cent few. It was not surprising that to him Communism appeared the better alternative, and it was easy for him to ignore the fact that most of Hong Kong's underprivileged population had fled from mainland China as refugees. His generation had the fire of youth and bitter grounds for their deep resentment. They offered the biggest danger, and paradoxically

113

deserved the least blame.

Watching him Barratt felt a moment of pity, for he knew where the blame really lay. The youth had run wild and was now a political criminal under arrest more through circumstance than through any fault of his own. The cause of his present hatred could be fairly evenly divided three ways. Partly it was the fault of the financial mandarins from Shanghai, the Chinese employers who owned the mills and the factories and exploited the masses by paying low wages to make cheap goods and large profits. Partly it was the fault of the British administration whose job was to govern and should not have allowed that situation to develop. And the final part of the blame lay with the Communist agitators who deliberately stirred up the whole festering mess simply to gain the propaganda victory desired by Peking.

Barratt realized slowly that he had no answer to make at all to the young riot leader and turned away. His men were still chasing off the last of the running rioters, and the fired car was beginning to burn itself out. Then the sergeant in command of mobile three came hurrying towards him and said bleakly:

"Superintendent, there is a dead man lying in the gutter beside the bus stop just down the road. I think he must have been attacked by the mob just before we arrived."

Barratt stared and then asked:

"How was he killed?"

"Clubbed to death, probably with fists and sticks." The sergeant wiped a trickle of sweat from the side of his face and added an opinion. "Perhaps he was waiting for a bus and they surrounded him. You know how they will corner a man and insist that he must kow tow before the red book of Chairman Mao. This man must have refused, and so they beat him to death."

Barratt turned for a moment to stare back into the expressionless face of the bespectacled mob leader who now sat quietly in the back of the Land Rover. Then he said bitterly:

"All right, Sergeant. I'll take a look at the body."

8

Bomb Blast

IT was an hour before dawn when Barratt checked out of Eastern and left the station in Chan's capable hands. Chan had been on duty for the past eighteen hours, but Barratt had been working for nearer twenty-four and had decided to give himself the first break. It had been a quiet night again after the remnants of the riot had been cleared up in Leighton Road, and the prisoners they had rounded up had all been charged with disturbing the peace and consigned to the cells. There was no one whom they could specifically charge with the bus stop murder.

The reports from the mainland side of the colony had again been quiet except for isolated incidents, and only two of those were serious. A bomb had been thrown across the street at Sha Tau Kok and had wounded one of the British soldiers who had been moved up to support the Gurkhas along the border, and another bomb had been exploded against the gates of a police station in Kowloon, but without causing any human damage.

Barratt knew that this was only the lull before the storm, and did not expect many hours sleep before he would have to be on his feet again. With luck the main demonstrations would hold off until the afternoon, but he would have to be back long before then to relieve Chan, who also needed rest.

He drove his own car, a Morris 1100, up to Hill Court on the western slopes of the Peak where he lived in a large, furnished flat. He parked the car in the basement garage and carefully locked all the doors. Then he took the lift up to the third floor and let himself in with his key. He moved quietly into the bathroom to wash and clean his teeth, the process took him ten minutes and then he moved into the bedroom. He was trying hard not to wake his wife, but the bedside lamp clicked on and he saw her blink open her eyes and smile sleepily.

"Hello darling, was it a busy night?"

"Busy enough."

He leaned over to kiss her, and noticed again with a feeling almost of humility the streak of premature grey in her hair. At forty-three Grace Barratt was still a handsome woman, and that streak of grey showed that although she never worried him for details of his job, she did worry *about* him, and he was aware that the grey had been getting more pronounced in the past weeks. When he straightened up she reached under the pillow to hand him his folded pyjamas and asked:

"Is there anything you want, John? Coffee or cocoa?"

He unbuttoned his shirt and shook his head.

"No thanks, love. Just sleep."

She watched while he changed into the pyjamas and then pulled back the thin covers on the bed so that he could slip in beside her. As he lay back she said:

"What time shall I wake you?"

He looked at his watch. "Give me five hours, say ten o'clock."

She smiled. "Ten o'clock, and breakfast will be ready."

She switched off the bedside light, and then leaned closer in the darkness to kiss him goodnight. His hand stirred and rested fondly on her arm, but already he was falling into sleep.

★ ★ ★

An hour later a bell shrilled sharply through Barratt's dreams. He groaned and shifted his shoulders across the bed, his hand reaching automatically for the telephone beside him. Grace switched on the lamp on her side, and then reached over him to take the phone from his hand.

"John, that was the doorbell."

He opened his eyes and looked at her, uncertain for a moment, and then he relaxed. Of course it was the doorbell, the telephone had a different note. He smiled and said:

"Sorry, love. I must be getting jumpy — and this is the only place I can afford to let it show. I'm not really as tough as I have to make the world think I am."

Understanding showed in her eyes as she put the phone back on its rest, and she said quietly:

"It has been a strain, hasn't it — these past few weeks? But the world is outside now, and you don't have to prove anything to me."

Barratt smiled faintly again and closed his eyes. He knew that he had found a real treasure in Grace. They had been together for fifteen years, and although it was childless he was convinced that their marriage was far happier than most. Grace had never tried to nag him, either to push him forward or to hold him back, and she rarely complained about her lot as a policeman's wife. All through his career she had allowed him to make his own pace, and now she was a warm, restful refuge where he could forget, if only briefly, the heavy responsibilities of a Divisional Superintendent. Barratt knew that a good woman could make a man, and a bad one could destroy him, and he had been very fortunate indeed. He had found the best kind.

He remembered the door bell and opened his eyes again, but her hand on his chest held him back.

"I'll go, they always telephone when they want you, so it's probably for me anyway."

Barratt felt too tired to lift his wrist, and turned his head instead to look at the bedside clock beside the telephone. The hands stood at six fifteen a.m.

"Who is likely to call this early?"

"I don't know but I'll find out."

Grace sat up and swung her legs

out of the bed, reaching for a dressing gown to cover her nightdress. Barratt closed his eyes again and began to drift back into sleep. Only one corner of his mind still retained the as yet unanswered question, why would anybody call this early? The ticking of the clock reminded him of the time, and the sound linked in his dulled memory with the earlier events of the evening. Weng Ki had helped to arrest a man who had planned to explode a bomb in City Hall. Another bomb had gone off in Kowloon and another in Sha Tau Kok. *Tick tock*, said the clock just by his ear, *tick tock tick*, just like a bomb.

The job was getting on his mind and he tried to supress his imagination. The bed creaked as Grace got up and found her houseshoes. He heard her go out of the bedroom and the question came back. Why would anybody call this early? *Tock tick tock* said the clock, refusing to be denied, and then another thought flashed through his mind. Grace had taken a long time to answer the door, but there had been no second ring of the bell.

Suddenly fear lanced through Barratt's heart like a shaft of lightning. He jerked away and kicked out of bed, shouting to Grace as he ran through the door. She had switched the light on and was just about to open the door to the corridor beyond the apartment when he shouted, and she turned back in surprise. Barratt grabbed her arm and yanked her back across the room. Nothing happened.

Grace stared at him and asked uncertainly:

"John, what — what is it?"

Barratt realized that he was sweating, and managed a weak smile.

"Nothing perhaps. I just had a horrible thought, and like I said before I'm getting jumpy."

They both smiled at each other, and then the bomb that had been left in the corridor outside exploded in a savage blast of sound and knocked the door down.

Barratt had instinctively grasped his wife and turned her away from the door, and they stood there shaken but unhurt. No longer were they smiling.

9

Shore Leave

THE *Carson City* was more than twice the size of the giant Cunard Queens, a floating war monster crewed by over five thousand men with a strike force of more than seventy assorted jet Skyhawks, Phantoms, Vigilantes and A-6 Night Intruders tucked away beneath her four and a half acre flight deck. She was one of the four great carriers serving rotation duty spells off the hot north coast of Vietnam, and three days previously her place of action had been taken over by the *Manhattan*. The crew of the *Carson City* were due for a turn of rest and relaxation. Their last R and R leave had been spent in Manila, and the one previous to that in Australia, but on this particular bright July morning the

126

carrier's anchors rattled down into the glittering blue sea outside the harbour of Hong Kong.

At noon the liberty boats started to ferry men ashore, and among one of the first cargos of eager US sailors was Lieutenant Marc Mitchell. Once they had scrambled on to dry land most of the sailors scattered in groups, either thirsting for girls and the bars, or heading for the tramway that would take them up to the Peak for a bird's eye view over the whole colony. Marc Mitchell fully intended to see all that there was to see, but for him there was a different standard of priorities. This was his first duty tour outside the United States and he was still sending batches of presents to the folks back home from every port. He was conscientiously aware that it was also getting pretty close to the old man's birthday, and so on this occasion the task of gift-hunting was his immediate concern.

He had been advised by more

knowing shipmates to do his hunting in Kowloon, where there were glittering bargains to be had in every shop window along the main Nathan Road. He took the advice and a five minute trip across the straits aboard the star ferry to the mainland city. By doing so he missed the violent mass demonstrations that flooded over eastern Hong Kong later in the afternoon. He knew nothing of the rampaging mobs who attacked many of his less fortunate fellow Americans, and chased most of them back to their liberty boats, or into the bars where some of the more courageous of the bar girls risked their own necks to drag the fleeing fugitives inside. He knew nothing of the pitched battle that was fought in the streets and in Victoria Park between thousands of rioting hooligans and the combined forces of all four of Hong Kong's police divisions in full riot order. He did not even know that all US Navy personnel were being advised to return to their ships. Kowloon had suffered the day before, and was now being allowed a breathing space while the more militant Communists flocked over to Victoria to help stir up the shifted scene of events. Kowloon was quiet, and Marc Mitchell shopped for his presents without meeting any hostile incident.

He walked the whole length of the busy, flamboyant canyon of Nathan Road which neatly bisected the pear-shaped peninsular and city of Kowloon down the middle. For his father he bought a bargain-price Rolex wristwatch, for his mother an oriental brooch carved out of pale green jade, and for his kid sister, seventeen years old and only four years younger than himself, he bought a bright yellow blouse of best Thai silk. He vaguely remembered that Sue had favoured yellow to match her blonde hair, and so naturally everything he choose for her was yellow. He found himself wishing that he could be back home in Philadelphia just for the few moments when they would be opening the parcels.

By the time he had finished his explorations of Nathan Road and most of the adjoining shopping arcades he was hungry. A Chinese restaurant with the name *The Great Shanghai* caught his eye and he went inside. He ordered Empress Chicken, which proved to be a thick and delicious chicken stew. Being American he also asked for a green salad and a beer, and coffee to finish. The Chinese waiter was long accustomed to the often conflicting demands of Americans and served him politely without comment.

When the young Lieutenant emerged on to the street again it was early evening. Dusk was near and the bar lights on the east side of Nathan Road were already winking their obvious invitation. However, Mitchell had arranged to meet a shipmate from the *Carson City* on Hong Kong side, and so he made his way back to the Star Ferry and the return trip across the straits. His presents were small and except for the parcel containing the silk blouse they were carried easily in his pockets, and so he had no need to return to his ship. He decided to go straight to his rendezvous, a bar called *The Golden Mandarin*.

If he had started to walk into Wanchai he would undoubtedly have been turned back by either the police or the US shore patrols, but this was his first visit to Hong Kong and even if he had had the inclination he did not know his way around well enough to consider walking. He looked for a rickshaw, for he quite fancied the idea of being towed royally around in true oriental fashion, but by chance there were no rickshaws available. He settled for a taxi, gave the name of the bar, and settled back to enjoy the ride. Now it was dusk, and the lights glittered like a million fireflies in the night.

As the taxi drove down Queen's Road East he began to notice the smashed windows, the damaged cars

131

and the litter of revolution along the gutters. The crowds had been dispersed and there was an abnormal number of Chinese police constables patrolling the pavements. The main waves of violence had now passed, and there were only occasional ripples left, but it was easy to see where the waves had been. The tense atmosphere that filled the city penetrated into the car, and after staring through the windows on either side for a few minutes, Mitchell asked dubiously:

"Say, what's been happening here? This place looks as though a bomb has hit it."

The Chinese taxi driver shrugged his shoulders.

"More troubles. There was a big demonstration here today. Yesterday there was big demonstration in Kowloon. The police killed two Chinese. Today the demonstration is to protest."

He could have warned the young American of what had been happening before starting the journey, but that way he would have lost a fare. Now they were almost there and the taxi had to be paid for anyway, and he added helpfully:

"Perhaps it is best if you do not stay here. Most US sailormen have gone back to ship."

Mitchell hesitated. "How far is *The Golden Mandarin*?"

"Here."

The taxi was already slowing to a stop, and the driver lifted one hand from the wheel to point out the head and shoulders of the pantomime chinaman shaped from tubes of yellow neon that hung almost above the car's bonnet. Mitchell held back a second longer, and then decided that Lieutenant Pete Pietowski might already be waiting inside. If there was trouble about then he could hardly leave a buddy waiting alone for him to turn up, and so Mitchell had to check it out. He shook his head at the taxi driver and then fished for his wallet to pay the fare.

"It's okay. I'm expecting to meet a

guy. Now that I've come this far I might as well go inside."

The taximan shrugged, accepted his payment as indicated by the clock, and frowned dubiously because there was only one HK dollar extra. Mitchell had been warned about taxi-drivers, but he was still young enough to be embarrassed and add another fifty cents. The driver smiled more cheerfully and Mitchell got out of the car.

The street showed no hint of danger, but Mitchell was prudent enough not to linger and went directly into the bar. A smiling Chinese girl held the door open and bid him a polite welcome. Inside all was quiet and subdued, and he realized after a moment that he was the only genuine customer. There were three or four girls sitting around one of the tables, and another girl leaning against the padded yellow leather bar talking to the barman, but that was all. There was no sign of Pete Pietowski.

Mitchell wondered whether his friend

had been delayed in getting ashore, or whether all shore leave had been cancelled. Pete would be cursing if it was, and so would a hell of a lot of other guys. The fact that the bar was empty of any US servicemen seemed to indicate that they were being kept clear of the area, and he guessed that it was only because the shore patrols had not noticed him in the taxi that he had passed through. However, Pete might yet turn up, and now that he was here he had only to make the return trip once. This place seemed safe enough, and he felt that he could afford to delay half an hour over another beer. If Pete came in they could take a taxi back together, if not he would take a taxi back alone before it was too late. He reckoned that he should come to no harm provided he did nothing stupid like wandering alone about the uneasy streets.

He moved up to the bar, sat down on one of the yellow-topped stools and ordered a beer. It was deftly served, and while the Chinese barman poured it from the bottle to the glass Mitchell found time to glance at the girl with whom he had been talking. She was very young, and wore a high-necked red *cheongsen*. She smiled at him, and moved her body slightly so that the slit skirt parted along her thigh. Mitchell answered the smile with a self conscious grin.

The barman placed the beer glass on the counter but appeared to be in no hurry either to be paid, or to resume his conversation with the girl. Instead he wandered away to the end of the bar and began to idly polish glasses. Mitchell took a pull at his beer, and then glanced sideways to find the girl glancing at him again.

Jenny Peng said a quiet, confident, and very friendly "hello."

Marc Mitchell said "Hi," and made a small salute, and at the same time searched his mind for something more original to follow up.

Jenny Peng had already made a

shrewd evaluation of the young stranger. The smart casual clothes, the slightly freckled face, and the college crew-cut hair-style practically screamed the definition of the All-American-Boy. She found them to be a stereotyped race, and it amused her to find that they in turn considered the Chinese to be undistinguishable and all alike. This one she guessed was probably an officer, for the officers were usually somewhat more reserved and better behaved than the ratings. Also he was a family boy. She had noticed the imprint of one of Kowloon's largest Thai silk emporiums on the wrapping of the small parcel he had laid on the bar counter, and the size of the parcel suggested a blouse or a jacket for 'Mom' or 'Sis'. It could also have been some saucy, embroidered lingerie for some Stateside sweetheart, but from the way he had averted his eyes from her exposed thigh she did not think that this one was yet bold enough to buy saucy lingerie. That would come later. Jenny Peng knew all the signs and was quite accomplished in the art of judging male psychology. She knew all the answers, yet she was wise enough to fill her dark almond eyes with innocence and still ask the questions.

"You are an American, yes?"

Mitchell nodded. "That's right, I'm from Philadelphia."

"And you are from the big ship, the one that flies aeroplanes?"

"You mean the *Carson City*." Mitchell grinned. "You could call it that, I guess. We call it an aircraft carrier. On board ship the boys call her Kitsville. That's after Kit Carson. He was an American pioneer when they first opened up the west. He fought indians and suchlike."

Jenny smiled. "Do you fly one of the fast jet aeroplanes? Are you a pilot?"

Mitchell shook his head. "No, I'm just an ordinary Naval Lieutenant. Just one of the guys who helps to sail the ship, and make sure that it's there when the sky jockeys come home to roost."

He took a sip from his beer and then realized what he was doing. He put the glass down and said hastily:

"Say, would you — will you have a drink with me?"

Jenny nodded. "Please, I would like that. A little whisky."

Mitchell called the barman over, and while the drink was being served Jenny hoisted herself discreetly up to the stool beside him. Behind his back she smiled with slightly malicious triumph towards the remaining bar girls who had only each other for company, and they either shrugged or smiled in return. When Mitchell turned to hand her glass she was attentive again and thanked him politely as she sipped her amber coloured fruit juice. Mitchell paid six HK dollars and fifty cents for his beer and the whisky. Jenny saw his brow furrow and spoke again to distract him from making the mental translation of HK dollars into the more familiar US variety.

"You must be a very brave man

to come into Wanchai tonight. Today there have been terrible riots. The worst that Hong Kong has yet seen. Many of your sailors were attacked and had to run back to the ship."

Mitchell grinned, and then suddenly realized that he was repeatedly grinning like a regulated monkey, and made the effort to change his face into something still friendly but more casual.

"I guess I must have missed all the fun. I've been on the other side of the harbour, Kowloon I think you call it. It was quiet over there. I didn't know there was trouble here until I saw the mess, and then a taxi driver told me something about it."

Jenny said seriously: "Perhaps you should go back to your ship. It is not safe for a US sailor to be in Wanchai tonight."

"It seems safe enough in here," Mitchell said. "And in any case I'm waiting for a buddy. He was on duty today, but we were going to meet here tonight to go over the town. Pete's been here before. He knows his way around."

Jenny shrugged. "I do not think your friend will come now."

Mitchell nodded thoughtfully. He too was becoming convinced that Pete must have been held up or turned back. Discretion advised that he too should return to the *Carson City*, but at the same time there was no threat here and he was attracted to the slim young Chinese girl by his side. She was so much younger and prettier than he had ever expected a bar girl to be. He wondered, like a hundred others before him, why she was here at all. Aloud he said:

"Like I told the taxi guy, I've only got to run the gauntlet once, whether I leave now or later. So, I might as well stay awhile. How about another drink?"

"Okay, but if you stay you must tell me your name. Mine is Jenny Peng."

Mitchell introduced himself as the barman served them again. Jenny turned a little closer towards him so that their knees almost touched and accepted her fresh drink with a bright smile.

"Thank you, Mark."

"It's Marc with a C," Mitchell said, and the self-conscious grin came back again. "That's my mother's way of trying to be different."

Jenny laughed and said: "Thank you, Marc with a C!"

She reached out and touched the parcel that lay on the counter and asked:

"This is a present for your girl in America?"

He shook his head. "No, that's for Sue — my sister."

Jenny looked sorrowful. "You don't have a girl in America?"

He shook his head again. "No serious girls anyway."

Jenny leaned forward and said confidentially:

"Tell me about the girls in America. Do you like the Chinese girls better?"

Marc Mitchell was getting out of his depth, but he persevered nobly. Jenny Peng knew how to titillate without scaring her fish away, and she played him like the expert female angler that she was. She knew full well what was passing through his mind. It was easier that he had no serious girl in America, but even so there would be a part of him that wanted to remain faithful to the idea of the American girl he would hope to have in the future. There would also be a part of him that was painfully aware of her own slim body and bare thigh, which would want to enjoy and possess her now. It was her task to ensure that the second part of him triumphed in the conflict within his mind.

They had several more rounds of drinks, and then although no more customers had arrived they moved to a more secluded table where Jenny could sit even closer by the American's side. Mitchell could feel her thigh against his own and her fingers caressing his arm. Her smiles never faltered, and when she leaned close he could smell the sweet fragrance of the perfume she had dabbed behind her ears. It was becoming hard to remember that she was a bar girl, and that to her he must be just another customer. It was more like she was a nice girl that he had just met, except he kept thinking about those ridiculous stories he had heard about Chinese girls. Pete Pietowski had told him that there was nothing in any bed in the world quite like a Chinese girl.

An hour passed before Mitchell remembered that he had meant to get out of Wanchai before the night became too far advanced. He waited for a break in Jenny's bubbling conversation, and then said half heartedly:

"I think perhaps I should be leaving. Maybe I can come back and see you tomorrow if there's no more trouble."

Jenny knew that it was time to be more business-like. She smiled and at the same time her hand moved under the table to rest lightly on his thigh.

"You can come back, Marc with a C. Anytime. But perhaps you like to come upstairs with me for a little while now. I have a nice room."

Mitchell hesitated, feeling suddenly overwarm and uncomfortable. There were words on his tongue but they were all jumbled up between reluctance and desire. He tried to think of Mom and Sue, but Mom and Sue were too many thousands of miles away, and Jenny Peng's lustrous eyes were gazing wide and hopefully into his own. Her hand began to gently move, stroking his leg.

"I think you are nice boy," she said softly: "I don't go upstairs with just anybody. I am a hostess, not a whore. But you I like. If you buy a bottle of whisky we can go up to my room."

Mitchell swallowed hard and then nodded.

Jenny smiled, and then stood up and led him over to the bar. The Chinese barman made no comment when she asked for the bottle of scotch whisky, and Mitchell paid quickly without questioning the exorbitant price. Jenny smiled again, hugged his arm against her side, and then led him through a draped curtain beside the bar. There was a staircase beyond and at the top a short corridor. She stopped at the third door, opened it, and ushered him inside.

It was a small room, simply furnished with a dressing table and a double bed. There was a small bedside table with glasses and a bottle of soda water on which she placed the newly-bought bottle of whisky, and there were some pictures of old china on the wall. Jenny closed the door, and then put her arms around Mitchell's waist and stood on tip-toe to be kissed. Mitchell complied, and then she stepped back smiling and turned her back.

"Please, Marc, the zipper goes down my spine."

Mitchell pulled the zipper down with unsteady fingers, and Jenny wriggled smoothly out of the red *cheongsen*. She stepped away from it and laid it neatly over the only chair, and then she slipped off her shoes and sat down on the bed and started to pour two whiskies. She wore only a bra, and brief panties of pale green silk. Mitchell began to undress, and when he was halfway through she brought him one of the glasses. She smiled at him once more and asked:

"Please, Marc, you like to give me a little money, yes?"

Mitchell felt embarrassed and picked up his jacket again. He found his wallet and peeled out a hundred HK dollars. He wasn't sure whether that was enough or too much, but Jenny seemed satisfied. She kissed him and put the money into a small purse on the dresser. Then she calmly unstrapped her bra and began to wriggle the silk panties down over her hips.

★ ★ ★

Jenny Peng had worked hard on Lieutenant Marc Mitchell for more than the usual reasons of her trade. He was American and an officer, and despite his youth he was one of the men fighting the Communists in Vietnam. She had made up her mind to take a grave risk when such a man came along, and she had decided that Marc Mitchell was the man. When he had dressed again she sat close beside him on the edge of the bed and said softly:

"Marc, there is something I wish to ask of you. Will you do for me a small favour, yes?"

Mitchell looked at her, and was surprised to see that her eyes were as earnest and hopeful as they had been when she had seduced him in the bar. There was something suddenly and unexpectedly vulnerable about her, and he could sense that her previous confidence and mastery of the situation had waned. He put his arm around her shoulders and gave her a small hug.

"Sure, Jenny. What is it?"

Jenny Peng passed her tongue nervously over her lips, still looking at him uncertainly.

"It is something that is perhaps dangerous, something that I cannot do myself. I want you to take something to the police."

"What sort of something?"

Jenny hesitated, and then got up and went to her dressing table. She pulled open the bottom drawer, taking the drawer itself right out, and from the cavity behind she produced a large sealed envelope. Mitchell helped her to replace the drawer, and then took the envelope from her tentative hand. He was aware that she was tense and afraid, and she glanced once over her shoulder to the door.

"Just this," he was puzzled. "What is it?"

"Please, Marc, it is dangerous to talk. The police will understand I think. Take it to them, but do not tell them that it came from me. You will promise?"

Mitchell hesitated in turn, but her eyes were pleading and finally he nodded.

"Okay, I promise."

She relaxed a little and then said:

"Thank you, Marc with a C. But now it is best that you should go. Take a taxi from here and do not walk in the streets. And, Marc, it will be best if you do not come back to *The Golden Mandarin*."

Mitchell stared: "But, Jenny. I want to come back. I want to see you again."

She shook her head and repeated earnestly:

"No Marc, believe me, it is much better if you do not come back."

10

The Blacklist

IT was the morning after the giant demonstrations. The tension had relaxed as though the whole of Hong Kong had subsided into spent exhaustion, and for the moment there was a lull of near normality. Inspector Chan sat at his desk at Eastern police station and wearily read down one of the first reports of estimated damage. The total cost of the whole series of riots was now running into millions of pounds, and he wondered almost bitterly how many resettlement housing blocks could have been built for the same price. There was no long-term sense in it all, but the pattern was the same the whole world over and there never was. Man was basically a stupid animal, ever willing to return to the wild whenever his little hates and fears were wound up to the right pitch, and there were always the smarter operators, the power-seekers and the petty politicians who were always eager to do the winding. Chan reflected sadly for a moment, and was not sure whether being a policeman had turned him into a cynic or a philosopher, and then he wondered was there any difference between the two.

He turned to the other reports that lay before him. Another man had been savagely murdered, a tram driver who had been repeatedly stabbed to death when one of the mobs had attacked his tram. In other incidents three buses and two cars had been set on fire by separate mobs, and one mob leader had been shot dead by a police patrol in Wan-chai. Thousands of stones and bottles had been thrown, and hundreds of tear gas shells and wooden anti-riot pellets fired. Throughout the day the police forces had been continuously shifted from one part of the city to another to deal with the fresh outbreaks of violence, and there was practically no part of Victoria that had escaped unscathed. The casualty list for Eastern Division showed eight constables injured, one of them seriously by a thrown bottle that had exploded in his face, and the reports from the remaining three divisions showed a similar average. Mercifully Kowloon had been quiet, and there had been no new incidents along the New Territories border with China where the Gurkhas still remained in control.

Chan picked up a final report, the total death roll over the past two days. The number now stood at eleven; five constables killed at Sha Tau Kok, and Constable Ho Kin murdered at Queen's Wharf; three riot-leaders shot dead, two in Kowloon and one here in Wanchai; and finally the two men murdered, the tram driver and the man at the bus stop the previous night. And what, he asked himself sourly, had it all proved or achieved?

While he studied the last report the intercom buzzer sounded on the desk. Chan pressed a switch on the box and said briefly:

"Inspector Chan here."

The voice of the station desk sergeant answered:

"There is a man here who would like to speak with you, Inspector, a Lieutenant Mitchell from the American Navy."

Chan sighed with faint exasperation. Life went on he supposed. No doubt Lieutenant Mitchell had been duped or robbed by some tout or some whore, and now he had come to complain. Tourists and sailors were forever looking for sins they shouldn't, finding them and suffering accordingly, and then coming to the police to right the assumed wrong. Or perhaps Lieutenant Mitchell had merely been caught up in yesterday's riots and had come to claim compensation for his bruises. In any case Chan had to see him. He said wryly:

"You may send him in."

"Very good, sir."

Chan heard the sergeant speak to the man in the outer office before he switched off the intercom, and then he sat back and waited. Almost immediately there was a tap on the door and then the sergeant appeared to usher in a young American with a lightly freckled face and crew-cut hair.

"This is Lieutenant Mitchell, sir."

Chan smiled and introduced himself as the sergeant went out, and then offered Mitchell a chair. He noted that there were no marks of a beating about the young man and discarded the possibility that he had fallen victim to one of the mobs. He said calmly:

"You are from the aircraft carrier, I suppose?"

Marc Mitchell nodded. "That's right, the *Carson City*."

Chan made a note on the pad beside him. He had not been pleased by the arrival of the American carrier because it could give the Communists fresh cause to stir up trouble, but he did not let the fact register on his bland face.

"What do you wish to see me about, Lieutenant?"

Mitchell hesitated, and then said awkwardly:

"I thought that all the officers in the Hong Kong police were British."

Chan smiled. "Only a few. Here only the Divisional Superintendent is English, but he is not here at the moment. I am the senior Chinese Inspector, and I assure you that you can speak quite freely with me."

Mitchell blushed behind his freckles. "I guess so, Inspector. I'm sorry if I managed to sound rude. I'm not used to dealing with policemen."

"I am pleased to hear that," this time Chan concealed his smile. "But why do you wish to see one now?"

Mitchell put his hand inside his jacket and drew out a large brown envelope. He passed it over the desk and said simply:

"I was asked to give you this."

Chan looked at him for a moment, and then at the envelope. There was no writing upon it and after turning it over once he reached for a paper knife to slit it open. He took from it two neatly typed sheets of paper and read them through briefly. When he looked up again he was frowning and he stared hard at the young American.

"Who gave you this envelope?"

Mitchell looked apologetic. "I promised that I wouldn't say. She said that you would understand what was inside, but that it wasn't important for you to know where it came from."

Chan noted the word she, but refrained from printing it upon his pad.

"In that case *when* did you receive the envelope?"

"Last night. I meant to come here straight away, but when I left the — " He stopped and made another awkward smile. "I mean when I started to come here, my taxi had to stop because of some trouble in the street. We turned

157

back and I went back to the ship for the night. I figured this morning would be soon enough. I hope I did right. Is it really important?"

"It could be. What time did you run into the trouble last night?"

"About ten o'clock, I guess."

Chan thought back. There had only been one disturbance reported around that time, and that had been a scuffle in Wanchai Road, which meant that the young American had been coming from somewhere in the bar district. He glanced down at the typewritten sheets again, and then faintly heard Barratt's voice bidding a brief good morning to the duty sergeant outside. He had not expected Barratt for another half hour, and he looked briefly at Mitchell.

"Excuse me please, I shall not be a moment."

Mitchell nodded and sat back from the desk. Chan got up and went outside, closing the door behind him. He walked down the corridor to meet Barratt and said calmly:

"Good morning, Superintendent, you're early."

Barratt said ruefully. "Morning, Charles. I couldn't sleep. Those damn workmen arrived again to finish putting up the new door at my flat. They started hammering and chattering so I got up and left. Grace was most annoyed."

"How is your wife?"

"She'll be okay. The shock is over, and I've given her a revolver and told her not to open any doors until she has identified the caller. She's a very courageous and level-headed woman, thank God." Barratt noticed the papers in Chan's hand and finished on a different note. "What's on your mind, Charles?"

Chan gave him the two sheets of paper.

"These were just brought into me by an American. He got them from a girl somewhere in the Wanchai area last night."

Barratt read silently down the long,

double-page list of names. At the top was the name of the Colony's Governor, linked with a price quote of £5000. The rest of the list included practically every official, either British or Chinese, in all of the main government and police departments, and again each name was linked to a price. His own name was there, valued at £800, and close below it Chan was quoted at £600. The average sum was £1000, and against six of the names there was a big black cross. Barratt looked up and said slowly:

"You know what we've got?"

Chan nodded. "The Communists have drawn up their own blacklist. They are prepared to pay those sums of money to anyone who can successfully murder any of the men whose names are upon that list. We have one such list, but I wonder how many others have already been circulated among our enemies."

Barratt grimaced. "Quite a few probably. I'm wondering what these black crosses mean against some of the names? The Police Commissioner for one, the Chief Justice and the Governor himself, and three others."

Chan was less sure, he rubbed his smooth jaw and suggested:

"Priority targets perhaps. The Communists may have appointed specific assassins to make the murder attempts."

"I have the horrible feeling that you may be right. In any case I'll get on to the Commissioner and make sure that everybody on this list is warned, and those emphasized in black are given special protection." Barratt tapped the list with his thumb and added. "It would be damned helpful if we knew when the attempts were to be made."

Chan frowned and hazarded a guess:

"The assassin's favourite hour is at night when he has the cover of darkness. Also the Communists will probably attempt to stage some kind of diversion to make sure that most of our forces are otherwise occupied.

I think that if there is to be a wave of assassinations then we should be on our guard when the next riots break out at night."

Barratt was inclined to agree again. "We'll do that, Charles, and in the meantime we'd better have another word with your American friend. I'd like to know where this list really came from."

"He does not wish to say. He made a promise to the girl."

"Did he now," Barratt said bluntly. "We'll have to see about that!"

★ ★ ★

Marc Mitchell looked up as the door opened and Chan returned. He saw that the Chinese was now accompanied by a heavy, rough-faced Englishman who also wore the starched shirt and shorts and the black-peaked cap of the Hong Kong police, and he had the sinking feeling that he was out-numbered and cornered. The big Englishman carried

162

the same air of hard authority as his own commanding officer, a leathery-faced Texan who had never been known to smile, and Mitchell guessed before Chan made the polite introductions that he was facing the top man. Chan remained standing but Barratt sat down behind the desk.

Barratt said. "I'd like to thank you for coming here, Lieutenant Mitchell. You may not realize it, but you have already helped us considerably — and I think you may be able to help us even more. You received this — " He tapped the list before him. " — from a girl somewhere in Wanchai, but I'd like you to explain in more detail if you will."

Mitchell looked at him and then to Chan.

"I didn't say anything about a girl, or Wanchai."

Barratt smiled. "You didn't spell it out, but Inspector Chan is a very perceptive policeman. I don't doubt that he would have gently milked a few more details out of you in time, but we may not have so very much time to spare. That's why I'm asking you to answer us more directly."

Mitchell looked embarrassed and tried to explain:

"I'd like to help you, Superintendent, really I would. But this girl was scared right out of her mind. She didn't dare come here herself, and she made me promise that I wouldn't give you her name."

"If she's scared, Lieutenant, then she's probably got good reason to be. We can give her police protection if you'll just give us her name."

"If I don't give you her name then she won't need police protection."

"Alright, just give us the name of the bar. We can keep a watch on the place without going near the girl."

Mitchell shook his head. He wasn't falling for that.

"If I give you the name of the bar then you'll soon find out her name. I can't do that either."

"But you did meet her in a bar? She was a bar girl?"

"Look, Superintendent, you're putting words into my mouth. I'm not going to answer any more of your questions."

Barratt studied the young American for a moment, and decided that despite his inexperience and his embarrassment the boy wasn't going to crack. His promise was his word, and there was a streak of stubborn loyalty in him that couldn't be shaken, not even when it was attached to a bar girl. Barratt changed his approach and indicated the double-page list in front of him. He said more quietly:

"Have you any idea what this really is, Lieutenant?"

Mitchell shook his head.

"No, I didn't open it."

"Then I'll explain it to you. This is a blacklist drawn up by the Communists who have been creating havoc in Hong Kong for the past three months. It's a list of all the men whom the Communists would like to see murdered, complete with prices quoting the bounty they are willing to pay for each killing. Naturally now that we know what is intended we'll place special guards over everyone on this list, which is probably all that your friend expected us to accomplish. She has already taken a grave risk by sending us this warning, but we still need to know more. In order to stop these threatened murders effectively I have to know who compiled and issued this list. I have to trace it back to its source, and the only way I can do this is through you, Lieutenant, and through the girl whose name you are holding back. We won't let the girl come to any harm, so can't you appreciate that this is more important than your personal promise?"

Marc Mitchell felt even more uncomfortable, and asked dubiously:

"Is it really as big as all that?"

Barratt nodded quietly, without taking his eyes from the American's face.

"It is, Lieutenant. Even apart from

the murder threat this could lead us to one of the main centres of Communist organization. Hong Kong has been virtually paralysed by strikes and riots for the past three months, and if we could break up just one of those main trouble centres we could be a lot nearer to bringing the Colony back to normal."

Mitchell was silent, and Barratt allowed him to think. At last the young man looked up and asked:

"How would you go about it, Superintendent — if I told you the name of the girl I mean? What would you do next?"

"Well first we'd have to talk to the girl. Obviously there are a lot of questions that we want to ask her."

"But if you go near that bar they might kill her!"

Barratt smiled and said: "We wouldn't be that clumsy, Lieutenant. We'll try and get the girl to come to us, or even better to meet us on some neutral ground. In fact you could help us there.

She knows you, and if you go back to her then perhaps you could persuade her to meet us somewhere. We'll settle for any time or any place that she cares to choose, wherever and whenever is safest for her."

Mitchell looked uncomfortable again.

"I don't think that she would agree to anything. She was very scared, and she asked me not to come back."

"But you could go back and try. And there's another thing, Lieutenant. If whoever owned that list finds out that it is missing then your girl friend could be in serious danger. Even now she could be in grave need of police protection."

Mitchell capitulated and said:

"All right, I'll try and help you. I'll go back tonight and talk to her."

"That's fine," Barratt relaxed. "But you could be playing with fire too, don't make any mistake about that. It's better for you both if you put me completely in the picture."

Mitchell hesitated for another moment,

but now it was too late to go back. He shamefacedly glossed over some of the more personal details, but in outline he explained all his adventures of the previous night, naming *The Golden Mandarin* and Jenny Peng.

11

City of Sampans

JENNY PENG was not pleased to see Mitchell return. She recognized his crew cut and freckles the moment he came through the door and looked hopefully for another customer to whom she could attach herself and ignore him. It was again early evening, and the other bar girls had already assigned themselves to the few sailors who had already arrived. There was no escape and she could only wait and smile bravely as he approached her table. His smile looked sallow in the dim light.

Mitchell said cheerfully: "Hi there! I was hoping to find you. Can I buy you another drink?"

It was impossible for her to refuse. It was her job to drink because that

170

was the way the bar made its profits. The barman was looking towards her and she knew that he would report any unusual behaviour to Madame Chong. She nodded unhappily and Mitchell went over to the bar and ordered a beer and a whisky. He came back with a beer and a yellow fruit juice, sat down beside her and said:

"Here's mud in your eye!"

"And in your eye too."

Jenny drank, and wished that the barman would look away. Finally the man did turn his head to attend to a bull-necked sailor who had his arm around another of the bar girls. The sailor and two of his friends were making a small but noisy party, and Jenny turned her face to Mitchell and said in a low voice:

"Marc, you should not come back here. I ask you not to come back."

"I know, Jenny." Mitchell matched his own voice to hers. "But this is important. I did the other thing you asked okay, but now they want to talk

171

to you. They think that you can help them a lot more."

"They?"

He nodded. "The p — "

Her hand gripped his wrist, almost spilling the beer from the glass in his hand.

"Please, Marc, don't say it."

He stared at her, reading the fear in her eyes.

"Isn't it safe to talk here?"

"No, Marc, it is not safe. Please go away."

"Okay then, let's — let's go up to your room."

"No, Marc. I can't go up to my room just like that. We have to have many drinks first. It is the house rule. And even my room is not safe. It is dangerous for both of us. Please, Marc, drink up your beer and go away."

Mitchell hesitated, and then tried again:

"Listen, Jenny, they're very grateful for what you did. But they think that you can tell them a lot of things that

172

they have to know. All they want to do is talk to you."

"But it is impossible." Fear was making her angry and she hissed the words. "There is no way I can help anymore."

"Jenny, they'll talk anywhere, anytime. There must be some-place where you can slip away for five minutes."

Jenny's heart was thumping and she was beginning to sweat. She was terrified that the barman or one of the other girls would overhear their conversation, or even worse that Madame Chong herself would appear from the curtains beside the bar. She said pleadingly:

"Marc, there is nowhere. You must go away."

Mitchell wasn't enjoying his task, he was beginning to feel like a louse, but he made one last persevering effort:

"There must be somewhere. Even if you live here in the bar you must go out sometimes."

Jenny was in despair. She was

sure that if they continued to argue in whispers then the barman would become suspicious and warn Madame Chong. There was only one way to stop Mitchell arguing and that was to agree to what he wanted. She said helplessly:

"Okay, Marc, I do as you say. But please stop talking about it."

Mitchell smiled a little. "That's fine. Where?"

Jenny sat for a moment, her thoughts flying like wild, frightened birds in her mind. Then she said:

"I have an aunt and an uncle who live in a sampan at Aberdeen. I visit them sometimes. I am going there tomorrow morning before the bar opens. Tell — tell your friends to watch for me there."

"What time?"

"About — " Her thoughts were so jumbled that for a moment she could not think. "Oh, about ten o'clock."

Mitchell said softly: "Thanks, Jenny. I'm sure you're doing the right thing, and if there's any danger they have promised that they'll protect you." He finished his beer and then said: "Now perhaps I'd better go like you said."

She gripped his arm again, aware that the barman had cast a stray and questioning glance in their direction.

"No, Marc, not yet. You must have more drinks. Talk normal for a little while. Then you must go."

* * *

"That's Aberdeen."

Jack Barratt slowed his Morris 1100 saloon as it rounded the headland on the western and seaward side of Hong Kong island and pointed ahead. Below the cliff road was a long, narrow harbour that was one vast city of floating junks and sampans, there were thousands of craft of all different sizes that almost blotted out the blue water sparkling in the morning sunshine. Beyond rose sheltering green hills, and at the landward end of the harbour a few white skyscrapers reared up from the fishing town of Aberdeen itself. To their right the sea glittered away to an obscure horizon where toy-like junks seemed becalmed in full sail.

Chan sat in the front seat of the car beside Barratt, and both policemen were wearing civilian clothes. To ensure the complete protection of the girl they had decided that it was better not to approach her either in uniform or from a police vehicle. There were far too many watching eyes and informers in Hong Kong. In the back of the car sat Marc Mitchell, and he stared dubiously down at the fishing harbour. He hadn't expected anything quite as cluttered and sprawling as this and said slowly:

"It's a bigger place than I thought, Superintendent. How do we find her in that lot?"

Barratt smiled ruefully. "It would have helped if you had got her to name some specific part of Aberdeen, or at least to give us the rough location of her aunt's sampan. But I think we'll manage. I doubt if she has a car of her own, so to get out here she'll have to use the local bus service. We'll drive down into town and park near the bus terminal."

The car began to accelerate down the hill, and through the passing curtain of tree branches on his right Mitchell could see fleeting glimpes of the wide, yellow quayside, broken up by strange square patches of indistinguishable white. Chan saw the interest in his gaze and explained:

"Those white squares are made up of thousands of fish laid out on wooden tables to dry. If you breathe deeply you can smell them even from here. Most of these people live only by fishing, or by hiring out their sampans to tourists. They are very poor and spend their whole lives upon the water."

Mitchell asked wonderingly: "How many people actually live down there?"

Chan shrugged. "We have never been able to properly count them. There are so many of them, they move from place to place, and the birth rate is so high."

Mitchell watched until the shops and restaurants of Aberdeen shut the masses of craft from view, and a moment later they had reached the small square where a few red buses were waiting to move out. There was a market street beyond and a hundred yards further on the edge of the harbour again. Barratt stopped the car where they could watch the arriving buses and glanced at his watch.

"It's nine-forty. We should be in plenty of time."

There was nothing to do but wait. The red single-deck buses arrived and departed at regular intervals, and Mitchell watched closely each time a batch of passengers dismounted from a bus that had appeared from the direction of Victoria. Jenny Peng was not aboard either of the first two buses, but when the third pulled into the terminal to disgorge its chattering load he recognized her slim figure among the last of the group. She was wearing a simple blue dress and dark sunglasses, and carried a covered basket over one arm. Mitchell pointed across the street: "That's her, Superintendent."

Barratt said calmly: "All right, Lieutenant, nip out and fetch her."

Mitchell got out of the car and hurried after the girl. When he had stopped her Barratt put the car into gear and moved up alongside. Chan leaned out of his window and employed his most friendly smile:

"Good morning, Miss Peng. If you and Lieutenant Mitchell would care to get into the car we can go for a short drive. That way nobody will see us talking."

Jenny Peng looked scared, but she nodded her head and allowed Mitchell to help her into the back of the car. The basket she set down at her feet and explained uncertainly:

"It is some food and presents for my aunt and my little cousins."

"Then we'll try not to detain you too long."

Chan smiled again, and after Mitchell had got inside and closed the door Barratt drove away. The car continued down to the quay where the sea palace restaurants floated like Chinese riverboats directly opposite, and then Barratt turned left. He drove the car about a mile outside the fishing town and then stopped along an empty stretch of the road overlooking the sea. He turned to find that Jenny Peng had removed her sunglasses, and that despite the comforting smiles of Mitchell and Chan she was still looking very nervous. Undoubtedly she had spent most of last night in worrying over the wisdom of keeping her unwanted appointment, and Barratt could guess at what was in her mind now. She was here only because she feared that Mitchell would return again to embarrass her at *The Golden Mandarin*, or worse, that the police would come there looking for her. He tried to put her more at ease and said: "You're a very brave girl, Jenny. I want to thank you very much for coming out here to meet us. My name is Superintendent Barratt, and this is Inspector Chan, and all we want is to ask you some questions."

Jenny's mouth was dry, but she nodded uncertainly.

Barratt smiled: "That's fine. Do you know what was in that envelope which you gave to Lieutenant Mitchell?"

Jenny nodded again and said slowly: "It was a list of names. Names of people I think the Communists want to kill. I did not understand it, but I think that if I send you this list then you can warn these people."

"We have done that, and we're very grateful for the warning. But where did you get the list, Jenny?"

She hesitated. "It came from — from Madame Chong."

"Madame Chong?"

"The Madame who runs *The Golden Mandarin*." Chan had the facts at his fingertips. "She also owns two other girlie bars in Wanchai, and I think there are more in Kowloon."

Jenny nodded more firmly. "Madame Chong is a very rich woman. She runs many bar places."

Barratt looked at her thoughtfully: "I see, but how did you get hold of this list, Jenny? Did Madame Chong give it to you, or did you find it, or what?"

"In one way Madame Chong give it to me, in another way I find it. Madame Chong give me a big pile of letters to take to the post. I walk to the post office, and when I get there I make sure that all the letters have stamps on them before I put them in the box. One letter has no stamp and no writing, it is not even sealed. I think that this letter has got mixed up with the others by mistake. Because it is not sealed I look inside, and I find the list. I post all the other letters but I keep this envelope and hide it in my room. I know I should take it to the police station but I am afraid. I keep it and wait. I wait for an American officer who I think I can trust!"

She looked almost bitterly at Mitchell as she finished and the young American blushed.

Barratt said: "What were these other letters you posted for Madame Chong? Were they all in the same kind of envelopes?"

"No, some were in little envelopes, some were in big ones. They were just ordinary letters. I have posted them sometimes before."

"Madame Chong must be a careful woman. How do you think the envelope with the list of names came to be mixed up with the ordinary letters?"

"I don't know. Madame Chong allows one girl to clean her office room. Perhaps this girl tidy the letters altogether and Madame Chong did not see. Perhaps — I don't know."

"All right Jenny, we'll leave that. But how did you know that the Communists mean to try and kill the people whose names are on that list?"

"I don't know for sure." Jenny fiddled uncomfortably with her sunglasses in her lap. "I only think that this is what the names mean, because of the sums of money that are marked beside each name. And I know that Madame Chong helps the Communists."

"How do you know that?"

"Because sometimes there are meetings, in the big party room above *The Golden Mandarin*. There have been a lot of such meetings since the Communists have tried to take over Hong Kong."

Chan asked shrewdly: "You don't want the Communists to take over Hong Kong?"

Jenny Peng shook her head, becoming earnest for a brief moment and forgetting her fears.

"No! I came from Red China when I was a child. It was a bad place. Hong Kong is bad too if you are very poor, but it is not as bad as Red China. The Communists killed my mother and my father."

Chan said quietly: "I am sorry."

There was a pause, and then Barratt resumed his questions.

"What else does Madame Chong do to help the Communists?"

"She — she tells them things. All the bar girls have to tell Madame Chong the little things they learn from the British and the American sailors. We have to tell what ship the sailors are from, where the ship has come from, and where the ship is going, all things like that. Madame Chong tells these things to the Communists. In *The Golden Mandarin* some of the bedrooms have peepholes, and if a girl goes upstairs with a man who has drunk too much and is talking interesting things then Madame Chong will watch and listen. I think it is the same in all of her other bars also."

Marc Mitchell had turned suddenly red, he said awkwardly:

"Was — was there a peephole in your room too?"

She looked at him, and his expression

caused her a faint smile.

"I do not think so, but I cannot be sure. It was a chance I had to take."

Barratt smiled briefly and asked:

"What sort of a woman is Madame Chong?"

"She is — she is a very hard woman. She is old, and she does not like men. I do not know why. Sometimes she frightens me."

"Do you know anything about her early life? Where she came from, and how she made the money to open her bars?"

"I don't know. I have only been a bar girl for a short time, and Madame Chong never talks about these things."

Barratt frowned for a moment and then asked:

"Jenny, do you know when the next wave of riots will take place? Have you heard anything from Madame Chong, or is there any talk among the other girls in the bar?"

Jenny was beginning to feel that she was talking too much, but she was committed and could not go back.

"There is some talk. I think that perhaps there will be more troubles tonight."

Barratt and Chan exchanged glances, and both of them were remembering their assumption that a wave of night violence would probably be staged to divert their attention from any assassination attempts. Then Barratt looked back to the girl and said:

"You've been a great help, Jenny, and now can you tell us everything that you can remember about Madame Chong and the people who come to these meetings she sometimes holds. Any little thing might be useful."

★ ★ ★

Jenny Peng talked for another half hour, and when Barratt was satisfied that he had extracted everything she knew he thanked her again, and then took out his wallet and removed forty HK dollars. There was a police fund for buying information, and he felt that the girl was far more deserving of a small cut than the usual level of informers with whom he had to deal. He said quietly:

"This is for you, Jenny, you can use it to buy some more presents for your aunt and cousins, and now we'll take you back to the quayside so that you can visit them in the ordinary way. We won't try to contact you again, that might be dangerous for you, but if you need any help or find out anything else that you want to tell us then you can always reach either Inspector Chan of myself at Eastern police station."

Jenny nodded in understanding, and after a moment's hesitation she took the money and put it away inside her handbag. At the same time she made a mental decision that in the future she would keep to the more profitable trade of selling her body.

12

Murder Night

DURING the afternoon reports began to filter in from the men of Barratt's floating ghost squad which verified Jenny Peng's warning. The hard-core agitators were out on the streets again, talking hotly to incite new demonstrations, and it became obvious that the Communist party bosses were hoping to whip up the most violent night of terror yet. In Eastern Division Barratt had as many of his men as possible out on patrol and had ordered a hard clamp-down on any gathering that could form the nucleus of a mob. The order had sparked a score of minor riots as the danger-groups were broken up and dispersed, and the hardworked police vans flooded the station with a constant stream of arrests. Most of the men brought in were young Chinese, furious political animals, spitting curses and Communist slogans at their struggling captors. Perhaps half of them were pure hooligans, but many were passionately devoted to their cause. They could see all too clearly the injustices and imperfections of their present world, but could not see that justice and perfection were an impossible dream. Like young men everywhere they could not yet compromise with reality, and believed that they could change the world for the better; and succeeded only in making their world an even bloodier mess. Their blind youth and high ideals made them perfect tools.

Again it was Chan who was left in charge of the station and the task of packing the belligerents into the already over-crowded cells. Barratt had to pay an urgent call to the Colony's Commissioner of Police. The deathlist that Marc Mitchell had brought from Jenny Peng had already been used to warn the men it had named, but now Barratt had to urge his own opinion that the coming night would include a mass wave of attempted assassinations. It was not a difficult case to argue with telephone reports constantly coming in to indicate that Hong Kong was boiling up into another explosion, and repeated warnings were sent to the men concerned, together with instructions to stay in their homes behind locked doors during the coming hours of darkness. The six names that had been specifically black-marked included the Governor of the Colony, the Chief Justice, the Colonial Secretary and the Secretary for Chinese Affairs. These were provided with a standing police guard outside their homes. The final two names were those of the Commissioner and Barratt himself.

The discussion in the Commissioner's office lasted for less than half an hour, for both were busy men. The Commissioner's safety was reasonably assured, for it was apparent that the night's events would keep him tied to his desk and the task of attempting to co-ordinate the efforts of the four police divisions under his command. However, Barratt's position worried him, and as the interview drew to a close he suggested bluntly:

"I don't think you should lead the patrols tonight, John. Everyone else on that list we can take steps to protect, and if you go out on the streets you'll be the only uncovered priority target. Stay in the station and let your Chinese Inspector do the outside work."

Barratt was human enough to hesitate for a second. He had led too many anti-riot patrols in the past week and here was a justifiably offered opportunity to escape the one that might well prove to be his last. He was tired and after the bomb blast in his own home his nerves had begun to show the first taut signs of strain. He did not think that he had revealed any outward signs, but inwardly he knew that the relentless pressure and long sleepless hours had started to take effect. He hesitated, but then said slowly:

"I can't do that. Chan has a price on his head too — not as high as mine perhaps, but high enough to tempt any street assassins who may be out hoping to get me. We've been taking our turns in station duty and leading the patrols, and tonight it's my turn on the streets. I won't send Chan out in my place.'

The Commissioner stared at him gravely for a moment, but decided not to press the issue with a direct order. He knew that Barratt was feeling the pressure, but the same could be said of any of the other Divisional Superintendents, and in fact of every officer, both British and Chinese, who made up the Colony's police force. They were all over-worked and weary, but also they were a well-knit team and so far had displayed a magnificent combination of firmness and calm. He did not think that any of his men would collapse, and had accurately pre-guessed Barratt's answer. It was merely reassuring to have his estimation confirmed. He smiled briefly and said:

"All right, John — but take care. Don't make yourself too easy a target." He paused and then added. "Do you think Grace would like to go over to my place and spend the night there. Neither of us are likely to get home before dawn, so she and Mary will be company for each other."

It was a good suggestion. The knowledge that Grace would not be worrying alone would leave Barratt with a clear mind to concentrate upon his own position, and both men knew it. Barratt nodded and said:

"If you're sure your wife won't mind."

"Of course not." The Commissioner smiled: "You know how she loves to talk. I'll send a car over to collect Grace."

★ ★ ★

194

Barratt drove his own car back to Eastern and had difficulty in getting through some of the mobs that blocked the streets. The mood was ugly and he drove with some urgency. The clampdown he had ordered had stopped any mass demonstrations from snow-balling throughout the afternoon, but he knew that the earlier disturbances had merely been a warming up. The main push would come with darkness. It was now dusk with the gaudy glitter of the neon signs flashing into life, and it was time to get his patrols on the move. Jeered curses and an angry waving of fists followed the course of his car, and then a thrown stone smashed abruptly through the rear window, scattering broken glass over the seat behind him. Barratt stamped hard on the brake and brought the car skidding to a stop. In normal circumstances he would have catapulted himself out of the car to chase the offender down, but now he checked himself in time and resisted that first impulse. The pavements were a mass of taunting faces, and neither his bulk, his authority nor his revolver would be enough to prevent him from being pulled down from behind. Since the death of Constable Ho Kin every man on the force had strict orders not to penetrate a hostile crowd alone, and he knew that it would be foolish to break that rule. The mob was already beginning to flow off the pavements toward the car and he slammed it back into gear and drove on. He knew that he would not have been able to single out the stone-thrower anyway, and cursed as a fusillade of fruit and vegetables grabbed from a nearby market stall were pelted against the boot of his retreating car.

He reached Eastern a few minutes later, and drove into the wide yard behind the station. The station's small fleet of Land Rovers were all ready to move out with the patrol crews assembled in full riot order. Chan was standing before them and indulging in a brisk preliminary pep talk. Barratt gave him a nod of acknowledgement, and then hurried into the station to pick up his steel helmet and tear gas goggles. He stopped to demand a brief report on the general situation from the duty sergeant at the desk, and then returned to take control over mobile one. Chan was impressing some quiet last-minute instructions upon the mobile's Sergeant, whom he had drawn a little to one side, but he broke off as Barratt approached.

"Everything is ready," he announced. "The men know what to expect and which areas to cover. Mobile one has Central District, mobile two Wanchai, and mobile three the Victoria Park area." He nodded towards Barratt's parked Morris with its broken window and added. "You had some trouble?"

Barratt explained and Chan frowned. They talked for a few more moments, and then Chan hurried into the station. Barratt swung into the front seat of the waiting Land Rover, and his driver briskly manipulated the gears to follow the other mobile patrols that had already roared out of the yard to take up their duty points. Barratt glanced back to check the faces of the men who made up his own team and make a brief acknowledgement. They looked grim but cheerful, a competent group of men of whom he could be justly proud. Their Sergeant was Sergeant Fong, now returned to riot duty by his own request after having been tactfully omitted from the duty roster for the past few days. The death of Constable Ho Kin was not forgotten, but the white heat of the Sergeant's anger had had time to cool.

The time was seven p.m., and Barratt chose to cruise back through the area where he had been stoned in his own car.

* * *

At seven thirty came an emergency request for reinforcements from mobile two to put down a mushrooming street

198

riot in Wanchai. Barratt arrived at speed to the familiar scene of more overturned cars blazing, and the air filled with animal howls and flying missiles as the mobs ran wild. The crew of the first Land Rover were hard pressed and had already suffered casualties as Barratt swung his own patrol into the fray. Mobile three arrived seconds later, closely followed by the large police van with its wiremeshed windows that was needed to convey the endless stream of arrests back to Eastern. The main street of Harcourt Road was an incredible confusion of running rioters and struggling police, mixed with swirling clouds of sparks and smoke from the blazing cars, and the acrid sting of bursting tear gas shells. To the inexperienced observer it would have been a hopeless exhibition of mass, spontaneous violence, but the police were by now grimly experienced in detecting the threads of command and hauling out the paid agitators and the hard core riot-leaders. The battle raged with fluid fury, moving up and down the length of the wide main road, or flowing in stormy waves up the intersecting side streets. On both sides men reeled away to the sidelines with broken heads or bleeding faces, and the night was hideous with screams and curses.

★ ★ ★

At eight-fifteen p.m., while the Harcourt Road battle was approaching its height, the police guard posted at the home of the Colony's Chief Justice intercepted a nimble young Chinese in the act of scaling the high brick wall that enclosed the back gardens attached to the house. The would-be-assassin dropped back into the road as he was challenged and took flight with two running Constables in pursuit. A third Constable blocked his path with a drawn revolver, but the youth was a fanatic who pulled a knife from inside his shirt and flung it hard at the Constable's face. It was a clumsy throw that knocked the peak of the Constable's cap aside without doing any further damage, but it gave the young Chinese the opportunity to duck past and continue his flight. The pursuing Constables fired three shots in an effort to bring him down, but the fugitive was moving fast out of range and sheer speed enabled him to escape.

* * *

At eight forty-five mobile one received an urgent call from Eastern that drew them off the Harcourt Road battle and brought them racing back into Central District where two constables patrolling on foot had been attacked by a gang of prowling thugs. As the Land Rover skidded to a halt the offenders scattered, leaving the two policemen bruised and beaten on the pavement. Barratt's men sprinted in pursuit with the grim-faced Sergeant Fong in the lead, while Barratt himself ran to help the fallen men. Both were badly shaken and bleeding from minor injuries, and he helped them into the back of the Land Rover. Fong and his men brought back three of the fleeing hooligans, and Barratt ignored the fact that the prisoners were now also somewhat battered and bleeding. All three of the apprehended youths wore red arm bands in imitation of Mao's red guards, and he felt no inclination to show them any sympathy. They were bundled into the over-crowded Land Rover and swiftly conveyed to Eastern. There Barratt paused only long enough to hand them over to Chan, and to ensure that the two injured constables received medical attention. Then mobile one was heading back to Wanchai to rejoin the battle there.

★ ★ ★

At ten p.m. the Wanchai riot was under control with the mobs scattered after three hours of continuous running battle, but at the same time came emergency calls from a neighbouring division that was struggling with an even larger mass demonstration further to the east at Victoria Park. Barratt left one mobile to cruise the Wanchai area and hurried the remaining three Land Rovers under his command to tackle the new outbreak.

* * *

Also at ten p.m. a group of three stealthily-moving Chinese in dark shirts and trousers approached the home of the Colonial Secretary. Their target was the large garage beside the main building that housed both his official and private cars, and they set to work silently to force the garage doors. While one man worked his companions kept watch.

They were allowed to complete their task, and not until they had opened the door and passed inside the garage did the waiting police cordon move in. The three Chinese put up a violent fight, but trapped inside the garage they had little hope of getting away. All three were overpowered and placed under arrest, and a Police Inspector took charge of the homemade bomb that they had hoped to place inside the Colonial Secretary's car.

* * *

At ten-five Barratt and his three mobiles arrived at Victoria Park. The scene that met them was a magnified repetition of the rioting they had only just succeeded in bringing under control. A huge demonstration of thousands of massed Chinese had gathered in the park to wave banners and hurl slogans, and had quickly started to spread outwards in a wave of violence. Hong Kong's remaining three police divisions were there in force in an attempt to contain the demonstration in the park area, and Barratt rushed his own patrols into the general mêlée.

The weary men hurried out from the three Land Rovers gripping riot sticks and carbines, and using their whicker shields to deflect the new fusillades of thrown stones and bottles. Tear gas and bursts of wooden anti-riot pallets were fired off into the crowd, and Barratt had to radio to Chan to send out more ammunition. His mind was fully occupied with the new job in hand, and he had forgotten that he might be in any personal danger.

* * *

At ten-fifty a third assassination attempt was blocked outside the Governor's private residence where the police guard arrested another determined young Chinese armed with a knife. The arrest was made after a violent struggle that left one constable with a savage gash in his upper arm that required eight stitches, and to end the struggle the would-be-murderer had to be knocked cold with a riot stick. The £5,000 bounty on the Governor's head was the richest prize of all, and two further attempts to claim it were made later during the night. Both were foiled with the more wary bounty-hunters making good their escape in the darkness.

* * *

At eleven thirty-five a two man team carrying another home-made bomb approached the home of the Secretary For Chinese Affairs, but were caught by the alert police guard long before they were in a position to do any damage. The bomb exploded as it was frantically thrown away into a neighbouring garden, but did nothing worse than to break a greenhouse window, tear up a bed of roses, and terrify a sleeping dog.

* * *

As midnight passed Barratt became optomistic that the Communists' planned murder night had become a complete failure. Chan had kept him informed via the radio of the nights events, and he had felt an increasing sense of relief as he heard that each attempt upon the lives of the men who had been black-marked for death had been checked in turn. The Victoria Park battle was also flagging and running itself to a standstill, and within another hour he knew that it would have burned itself out. He was aching with weariness in every bone, and he knew that the men under his command were just as tired, as were the men from the other divisions battling beside them, but the rioting Chinese were also exhausted by their efforts, and were beginning to disperse.

It had been another bloody and busy night, and the last of the defiant ringleaders were being rounded up and packed into the police van on the first lap of their journey to the cells, and Barratt was beginning to relax. He stood by mobile one with the radio microphone in his hand and exchanged a few more words with Chan to describe the present situation. Then he moved away to a patch of higher ground to watch the last of the mopping-up operations. His men needed no directions or supervision, and he felt that he could stand apart and breathe more easily.

He didn't see the tense-faced young Chinese in the faded blue shirt and trousers who circled cautiously round behind him. He stood with his revolver holstered and his hands resting on his hips, his feet apart and his back making a broad and inviting target. The Chinese edged closer, his whole body quivering and his eyes glittering with a mixture of greed and hate. He was undecided, but Barratt was momentarily separated from his men, and around them there were streams of spent rioters hurrying to exit from the park. By weary mutual agreement the tumult was over, and the police who already had their hands and their cells full, were allowing the stragglers to leave unhindered.

The Chinese with his eyes fixed upon Barratt's back made up his mind suddenly. He pulled a switch-bladed knife from his pocket, thumbed open the blade, and rushed forward to stab it between the Englishman's broad shoulders.

Barratt heard the patter of desperate feet across the dirt and swung round to face his danger. He was caught off-balance, slipped and started to fall, twisting to one side. The Chinese made a last bound like a leaping cat and lunged with his knife, and in the same second a police .38 barked savagely from his right. The young Chinese was knocked spinning in mid-air and his tight-clenched, hating face became a scream. He fell in a heap and lay writhing with blood staining his shirt just below and behind his right armpit. Barratt straightened up slowly, and then Sergeant Fong came running across with his drawn revolver still cocked in his hand. By the time Fong had ran the few steps the man he had shot had stopped moving and was dead.

Barratt swallowed hard, and brushed dirt off the side of his shorts where he had fallen. He said grimly:

"Thank you, Sergeant — I think he would have had me if you hadn't stopped him in time."

Fong nodded, and replaced his revolver in his holster. He did not tell Barratt that he had received explicit instructions from Chan before the patrols had left Eastern station, and his orders had been to cover Barratt's back throughout the night. Barratt had forgotten his own danger, but Fong had been watching him like a hawk.

13

Recriminations

THE aftermath of the dark wave of terror and attempted assassinations was a bright but subdued day of uneasy calm, All those who had taken part in the savage street fighting, police and rioters alike, were in need of sleep and rest, and so there was an unspoken but mutual truce. The police who remained on duty were still busy sorting out arrests and making charges and the courts worked overtime; while the Communist leaders also needed a respite to tally up their gains and losses, and to think about their next moves. The ruined and refuse-littered streets bore sorry witness to what had happened, and the whole island seemed to tremble in the mid-summer heat while its inhabitants took stock of the havoc they had wrought. Traffic moved slowly, and most of the shops and bars kept their doors closed.

It was late afternoon when Madame Chong received her summons, and her sour face wrinkled even further with displeasure. If it were possible she would have ignored it, but the message came from Lee Kung, and she knew she could not refuse. She could not even vent her feelings upon the messenger, for that might be interpreted as indiscipline towards the tall party man who had sent him to her, and so she found cause to thrash one of her luckless bar girls instead. Her trade was disrupted and she expected no customers for the next few days, so it did not matter that the girl's young body bore a scattering of weals and bruises.

Later in the evening she called a taxi to take her to the large trade union building where she had been instructed to attend. Lee Kung had moved his headquarters here, despite the fact that it was under constant police observation and therefore lacked the greater security of the *Golden Mandarin*. Lee Kung's ego demanded that he meddle in the centre of operations, and he still considered it beneath his dignity to stay hidden in a brothel, and after the first two days following his arrival he had insisted upon the change.

Now Madame Chong felt uneasy in mind as she paid off the taxi and hurried into the building. In her opinion Lee Kung was taking an unnecessary risk in calling a meeting here instead of at her own unsuspected premises where all the previous gatherings had taken place, and she did not care for unnecessary risks. She was not sure whether Lee Kung was acting with blind arrogance and allowing his own conceptions of personal and party dignity to influence him in discarding the *Golden Mandarin* as a rendez-vous, or whether he was deliberately trying to stress to her that she was under the shadow of his disapproval. There had been friction between them, and their mutual dislike, although unspoken, had intensified. Lee Kung was accustomed to fawning and humility, and had received none, and Madame Chong had found him even more detestable than most of the species she hated. Either way she did not like the way that events were developing.

She had arrived early, knowing that to arrive even a fraction of a minute late would be viewed with sharp displeasure, but even so most of the party officials and organizers who had shared her summons had taken their places before her. Here there was a large conference room specially provided for the normal union consultations, where the familiar faces who had so often congregated in her more comfortable rooms were now arranged around the large table. On the walls were two or three large framed photographs showing various aspects of Chinese industry, and a large, benignly-smiling portrait of Mao Tse Tung, complete with a golden halo radiating around the great Chairman's head.

Madame Chong was acknowledged by a curt nod of welcome from Lee Kung, who stood scowling by the only window that looked out over the street. Then the tall man from Canton turned his back to the room again and ignored them while the old woman in black took her seat. The men around the table also acknowledged her with brief words or an expressionless inclination of the head, but she did not bother to answer them. It disgusted her to see that they showed so much fear to the mere presence of Lee Kung.

The last man to arrive was the financial expert from the Bank of China, who was still reasonably safe in the knowledge that his part in all their efforts could show no fault. When he was seated Lee Kung took his own place at the head of the table, although he remained standing. The hands of the clock stood at seven fifty-five p.m., five minutes before the meeting had been scheduled to start, but now that they were all assembled Lee Kung wasted no time.

His opening speech was a solid thirty-minute stream of vituperation and abuse. He cursed and ranted with a fury that was fired by his own inner fears, for he knew full well that every atom of wrath that he poured upon their heads would be returned two-fold upon his own when he made his personal report to Peking. He hurled accusations of failure, treachery and incompetence at them individually and *en masse*, and threatened them with wholesale deportation back to China. His dark angry face grew flushed with the heat of his words and emotions, and ultimately his ravings became incoherent and forced him to come to a stop. He sat down still quivering with rage and worked out the last of his passion by beating his clenched fist repeatedly on the table.

When at last he was silent the silence was absolute. No one had dared to speak or move while the torrent of criticism and recriminations had flowed around them, and no one dared to speak now. A minute passed, and then Lee Kung had recovered himself sufficiently to glare around the table again. Most of those present kept their heads bowed and stared blankly at the table before them, but the old woman in black still sat stiffly erect, her dark eyes unflinching in the wrinkled mask of her face.

Lee Kung clamped his teeth to hold back a new flood of abuse. He knew that he would lose face if he proved himself capable of nothing but continuous remonstrations and he had to struggle within himself to become more practical. He said harshly:

"It was your plan, Comrade Chong. You assured us that enough of their senior officers and officials would be murdered under the cover of last night's riots to rattle the police forces into taking Chinese lives. But no one was murdered — not one attack was successfully carried out — and only one rioter was shot dead. It was not enough. Why did you fail?"

Despite herself the old woman could feel a tremor of fear in her heart. She despised the man who pointed the finger of accusation towards her, but she could not ignore the power that he could wield. Also she was more fully aware than most that they had fermented what was most probably the last really large wave of violence that would break over the long-suffering colony. The masses in the streets on whom they relied to carry the brunt of their attacks had grown weary, and the limits of their enthusiasm had been reached. From now on there could only be a decline in the disorders and riotings, and soon the price of failure would have to be paid in Peking. Madame Chong hoped that she still had sufficient value here in Hong Kong to save her from the backlash of Peking's wrath which would almost certainly topple most of her companions at the conference table, but first she had to absolve herself from any direct blame. She kept her hate controlled and answered carefully:

"Only the plan was mine. It was a good plan, but I was not responsible for ensuring that it was carried out. It was not my task to organize the demonstrations, or to select and direct the men who were to take the lives of the imperialist dogs we had sentenced to death. The failure to achieve our aims cannot be brought back to me."

Lee Kung glared at her across the table, she knew that he dearly wanted to hold her responsible but her arguments held truth and added frustration to his anger. For a moment they held a hostile clash of eyes, and then abruptly Lee Kung turned his head to single out one of the union leaders on the opposite side of the table.

"You, comrade Hing! You were responsible for planning the demonstrations! Why did they fail?"

The man addressed looked up warily.

His face was a pale moon behind rimless spectacles, and his lips were thin and colourless. He said precisely but warily:

"There was no failure in the demonstrations. My organizers performed their task well, we had over four thousand rioters out on the streets, at Wanchai and at Victoria Park. We engaged the police forces and kept them busy for five hours. That should have been more than sufficient. The fault lies with those who should have performed the assassinations."

There was another moment of cold silence, and then Lee Kung asked harshly:

"Then who is responsible?"

Hing did not look at any of his colleagues, but kept his gaze focussed on an area of blank wall just above and behind Lee Kung's head. He said slowly:

"Comrade Weng had the particular task of selecting the men who were to kill the British officials whom we had expressly named."

Lee Kung shifted his gaze further down the table. Weng was another union official, a thin man with a flat forehead that turned sharply back beneath slicked black hair. He stirred uncomfortably in his seat, but like the others before him defended himself with carefully chosen words.

"It is true that it was my personal task to plan the executions. I selected the men who were to make the attempts and gave them their instructions. I picked the best men available and gave them all the assistance that it was possible for me to give. We failed because every single man we had marked down was being closely guarded by the British police. Such strong guards have never been posted before throughout the three months that we have been conducting our campaign, and I can only believe that the British were warned. Not one man on the death list that we prepared left his home last night, and those to whom I had assigned specific assassins were all well protected. Someone has betrayed us."

The last sentence was a stone cast into a pool of silent fear. The unseen ripples radiated softly through the room while every face remained still and unblinking. Hing was the first to speak, and his voice held a note of dissent:

"If we have been betrayed, then why have the police refrained from raiding this building?"

Weng turned his head to face his accuser. He knew that there had to be a scapegoat for their combined failure, and it was clear that Hing had nominated him for the role. Weng was afraid but far from panic, he said firmly:

"The police will not raid this building because they dare not. They have known throughout that most of the demonstrations were organized from here, but until they have absolute proof they will hesitate to raid a trade union H.Q. To take direct action against the unions would be bad politics for them."

"But if we have been betrayed, then they would have the absolute proof of which you speak."

Weng was arguing upon weak ground, and in the face of Hing's insistence he retreated back to his strongest point. He leaned forward and repeated:

"The fact remains that the British were warned. Every man whom we had marked down for execution was given police protection. Without those extra police guards the executions would have been carried out."

Hing was prepared to continue their private argument, but Lee Kung choose to interrupt. He said flatly:

"It cannot be coincidence that the men who headed our deathlist were given additional protection while the demonstrations of last night were taking place. Either we were betrayed — or a copy of that list has passed into the hands of our enemies."

Hing smiled with faint triumph and said softly:

"One copy of that list was circulated

to each person here. I can account for my copy. Only Comrade Weng received extra copies to ensure that the word was spread down through the lower levels of administration."

Weng shifted uncomfortably, knowing that he was still isolated by the shadow of suspicion. He said quickly:

"I received six copies of the list. One I retained, but the others were passed to my subordinates. It was necessary that details of the rewards offered should be widely known if they were to serve any purpose."

Lee Kung said with finality:

"Enough of this. Eighteen copies of that list were printed. They will all be returned to me. If there is anyone who cannot account for the total number entrusted to him, then we shall know where the fault lies."

There was no more argument, and Hing and two others were immediately able to open their briefcases and return their typewritten copies of the deathlist across the table. The meeting was adjourned until the remaining copies could be gathered in.

★ ★ ★

Madame Chong made her way directly back to the *Golden Mandarin* and hurried to her room. She had no real fear that her copy of the list might prove missing, but she knew that it would be wise to return the two typewritten pages as promptly as possible. She checked quickly through the more important papers that were locked in her private safe, and then experienced the first small shock of doubt. She turned to her desk and searched hastily through the papers there, and by the time she had searched them twice doubt had crystallized into a sharp fear.

For a moment the old woman stood very still in the centre of the room, thinking hard. No one had access to her room except the one girl who cleaned and kept the place tidy. She rang a small bell to call the girl to her, and while she waited removed the black snake of the whip from her bedside drawer.

The cleaning girl came promptly, but protested her innocence despite savage questioning and a few experimental cuts of the whip. Madame Chong felt inclined to believe her, but even so the deathlist had been left here in her apartment, and the fact that it was not here now meant that someone had removed it. Her own skin was at stake, and filled with a violent determination she descended to the bar to consult her head barman. It was part of his job to keep a watchful eye upon the bar girls she employed, and as all the girls lived upon the premises it proved an easy task. The violence of the past few days had caused the girls to stay close even during their off duty hours, and within the past two days since the list had presumably disappeared only two girls had left the premises for any length of time.

Madame Chong questioned the two frightened girls in turn. The first girl had gone to visit some friends and had been absent for an hour. Madame Chong sent her barman to verify the story, and he returned after half an hour to report that it was true. The second girl was Jenny Peng, and Jenny had been absent the previous morning for almost three hours before the bar had opened at noon.

Wretchedly Jenny explained that she had gone to visit her aunt at Aberdeen. It was a frequent excursion of hers that should not have warranted any suspicion, but there was no one else upon whom suspicion could fall, and so Madame Chong again despatched the barman to investigate the tale.

After an hour the man returned. He had found and talked to Jenny's old aunt on board the sampan at Aberdeen, and the unsuspecting old woman had frankly admitted that her niece had only paid her a short visit of less than half an hour. The journey out to Aberdeen took approximately twenty minutes by bus, plus a further twenty minutes to return, and so simple arithmetic left well over an hour of that morning for which Jenny could give no satisfactory account.

14

Search for Jenny

IT was eleven a.m. of the following morning when the third liberty boat of the day tied up at the U.S.A. servicemen's landing at Wanchai. Marc Mitchell had missed the first two boats, for his duties had kept him aboard the *Carson City* throughout the early morning, but now he hoped to be the first man ashore from number three. As it happened he made fifth place, for the boat was packed with sailors whose eagerness matched his own, although almost certainly for different reasons. Most of the sailors dispersed in pairs or in groups, but Mitchell hurried off alone.

It was another brilliant day, with the sunlight striking back off the waters of the harbour to dazzle the eyes.

The traffic was running more freely with taxis and rickshaws out on the streets again, and Hong Kong had returned to near-normal. The streets had been partially cleaned and the tangled skeletons of the burned out cars taken away, and it was mostly in the broken glass and boarded windows that the last traces of the riots could still be found. Life and pedestrian traffic filled the pavements once more, and Mitchell had to weave his way through the crowds. A hopeful rickshaw boy tried to claim his custom, but Mitchell waved the man and his red-painted carriage away. The *Golden Mandarin* was not a long walk, and by now he was familiar with the route he had to take.

When he reached the bar he hesitated before going in, standing for a moment beneath the blank, unlit sign of the old pantomime chinaman. A nagging voice of caution told him that he should stay away rather than take the risk of compromising Jenny Peng any further, but balanced against that one voice of caution were conflicting ties of loyalty and feeling. Jenny had risked much in trusting him, and to a certain extent he had betrayed that trust, and now a vague guilt complex made him feel responsible towards her. Common sense would insist that he could serve her best by avoiding the *Golden Mandarin*, but common sense was over-ruled by a strong reluctance to abandon her completely without first ensuring that she was in no definite danger. Also the *Carson City* was due to sail in two days time and this might prove to be his last spell ashore, and consequently the last opportunity that he would have to see her again. And underneath all his awkward worries and fears on her behalf there was the simple, basic desire just to see her once more. She was not the first girl he had made love to, but there had been very few before her and he was still too young to discard her lightly. Even though he had paid for her she had still been sweet and warm towards him. However, he had argued all of this in his mind before he had left the *Carson City*, and after a brief initial pause in the doorway he went inside.

The bar had only just opened for business, and he was the first customer. None of the bar girls were in evidence, and there was only the Chinese barman reading a newspaper behind the bar. Mitchell faltered again, undecided whether he should come back later, but then the barman looked up and saw him, and laid his newspaper down. Mitchell decided to stay and walked across to order a beer. He stood against the bar, ignoring the yellow-topped stools, and glanced casually around while his beer was being poured. He was hoping that Jenny would appear from one of the curtained doorways behind the bar, but the doors remained closed and the curtains did not move. The beer was placed before him and Mitchell fumbled in his pocket for his loose change. As he paid he said casually:

"It's quiet in here. What time do the girls start work?"

The slit eyes regarded him for a moment, and then the barman answered shortly:

"Anytime."

The one word was neither helpful nor encouraging, and Mitchell seemed to remember that the man was normally more friendly than this. He sipped his beer and tried again:

"Will Jenny be in today?"

"Jenny?"

It was a blank question mark that made Mitchell feel uncomfortable. He said more bluntly:

"Jenny Peng — she works here."

The barman shrugged and then said flatly:

"Not today."

As he spoke he picked up his newspaper and deliberately turned away, opening it up again to continue his reading. Mitchell watched him uncertainly and tried to suppress a feeling of angry frustration. He wanted to see Jenny badly, but he did not want to make the mistake of being too persistent in his enquiries. The barman's attitude had him neatly checkmated and he didn't know what to do next. He drank slowly at his beer, his brain ticking over with renewed doubts and fears, and wondered how long he could afford to sit around the bar in the hope that Jenny might eventually appear. His glass was becoming empty, and he tried to calculate whether there would be any point in re-opening the conversation with the barman when he re-ordered, and then there was a movement behind one of the curtained doors to his left.

Mitchell turned his head hopefully. A young Chinese girl in a blue *cheongsen* emerged from behind the golden curtain, and for a moment a smile was born on his face. Then he saw that it was not Jenny but another of the bar girls, and the smile faded again. He looked back at his beer, but the girl came and sat on the bar stool immediately beside him, and when he glanced up she gave him a bright smile.

They both said hello, and Mitchell felt flushed and uncomfortable. He didn't want this girl, he wanted Jenny but after a moment it occurred to him that at least this girl might be more communicative than the poker-faced barman. He drank the last of his beer, and invited the girl beside him to join him in another drink. The invitation was promptly accepted, and while the drinks were served the girl introduced herself as Betty Sing.

Betty was small and dark with bright, almond-shaped eyes and a ready smile, and her body was shapely enough to be tempting if Mitchell had not been so obsessed with his concern for Jenny Peng. He allowed her to talk politely for a moment, answering the preliminary questions about himself and his ship, but when she remarked that she had seen him before she gave

235

him the opening he needed to turn the conversation his own way. He admitted his previous visits to the *Golden Mandarin* and then went on:

"The last time that I was here I talked with another girl, her name was Jenny Peng — do you know if she will come in today?"

Betty Sing shrugged her small shoulders and said sadly:

"I am sorry, but Jenny Peng does not work here anymore."

Mitchell stared at her, distrusting the look of apology that she had conjured on to her face but finding himself unable to read anything behind it. He said slowly:

"But she was here two days ago, what happened to her?"

"I think she went to another job."

Again the shrug, and then a brief smile. Betty Sing touched her hand to his knee, squeezed gently and added:

"It does not matter, I will be your girl friend now."

The dark, nameless uncertainty was

growing in Mitchell's mind. He barely felt the pressure of her fingers on his leg and he was only aware of the fact that something was badly wrong. He knew that the barman who stared steadily at his newspaper was listening to every word, but that no longer seemed important. Mitchell tried hard to read something, anything, behind Betty Sing's bright smile, and then asked:

"What kind of a job? Where did she go?"

"I don't know."

The girl shrugged her shoulders again, and Mitchell was beginning to find the repeated, empty gestures annoying. He said persistently:

"But wasn't she a friend of yours?"

Betty nodded brightly:

"Yes, but she did not tell me where she was going. I only know that she has found another job, and that she has left. She went yesterday."

Mitchell wanted to press the matter further, but he knew that he would get nowhere. Instinctively he knew that Jenny was in trouble, and that already his presence here must have done more harm than good. He too shrugged as though it didn't matter, and forced a smile on his face as he took a tasteless drink from his glass. Betty's hand was still on his knee and she leaned forward more heavily to murmur:

"Why don't you come upstairs with me, and forget Jenny Peng? I can give you much better time!"

Mitchell remembered what Jenny had told him of the house rule; that the bar girls were expected to keep their customers drinking as long and as expensively as possible before allowing any satisfaction of their sexual appetites, and Betty Sing's undue haste to distract his attention from her predecessor was another ominous sign. Betty continued to stroke his leg, but all that Mitchell wanted now was to disentangle himself and get away before he made any more blunders. He drank his beer and then made his excuses to leave.

* * *

Once he was outside the *Golden Mandarin* he walked briskly, but only until he reached the next street. There his pace slowed to a dawdle as he tried to think. A minute passed as he walked slowly and aimlessly, his brain worrying at the problem of where Jenny might be, and then abruptly he decided upon a course of action and ran to catch a passing tram. It would be dangerous for Jenny if he were to make any further enquiries at the *Golden Mandarin*, and he could only think of one other possible source of information. The tram took him into Hong Kong's Central District and when he stepped down into the streets again he had only a short walk to the bus terminus opposite the vehicular ferry pier where he caught a bus to Aberdeen.

He sat impatiently through the short, twenty minute bus ride that took him round to the seaward side of the island, barely noticing the crowded bustle of the passing streets, and unimpressed by the fine, sweeping views over the harbour as the road circled around the bulk of the peak. On his previous visit he had found time to admire the picturesque scene as the road finally wound down into the fishing village with its colourful harbour packed with its teeming maze of junks and sampans, but he found no time now. When the bus stopped he got out quickly and hurried down to the harbour's edge.

He was remembering the meeting he had arranged between Jenny Peng and Barratt and his Chinese Inspector. After the two policemen had extracted all the information that was possible from the girl they had brought her back here, but after she had left the car Barratt had lingered to watch the direction of her next movements. Mitchell knew that the burly Englishman had marked down the sampan that Jenny had visited with the small basket she had carried to her aunt, and now the young Lieutenant was trying desperately hard to remember which sampan it was. He had not taken such particular notice as Barratt, but he felt certain that Jenny had been taken out to one of a group of jumbled sampans that lay beyond the decks of a line of large junks moored almost immediately at his feet. He stared towards them, and wished that all the hundreds of sampans in the harbour didn't look so hopelessly alike, but even so he felt that he could remember Jenny going aboard one of the nearer sampans in that particular group.

While he was still trying to bring the memory more clearly into focus a Chinese woman with a large straw hat and a small baby tied to her back came up beside him. She smiled hopefully and asked:

"You want sampan — go round harbour?"

Mitchell pointed to the group of sampans that held his interest and explained:

"I want to go out there. Will you take me?"

The woman nodded cheerfully:

"I take you all round harbour. See floating restaurants — see everything. Ten dollars for one hour — okay?"

"Five dollars," Mitchell said: "I only want to go across to those sampans."

"Five dollars, half an hour."

There was a faint suggestion of disappointment that he would not take the full tour, but the sampan woman was still cheerful. Mitchell realized that it would be easier to direct her once he had embarked than to attempt to explain exactly what he wanted now, and so he nodded and said "okay." The woman smiled and then led him a few yards along the edge of the quay to where a very rickety flight of green-slimed board steps led down to the water. Her small, flat-bottomed sampan was tied to the foot of the steps, and she went down quickly and easily despite the baby strapped to her back. At the bottom she held the rocking sampan until it steadied, and then smiled to invite Mitchell aboard. The young Lieutenant stepped gingerly, although the steps were not as slippery as they looked, and the sampan woman steadied his arm as her clumsy craft rocked again under his added weight.

Mitchell sat in the double seat in the front of the sampan while the woman quickly untied the single mooring rope. She pushed the sampan away from the quay and as they slid out into deeper water she used one hand to work the long steering oar at the stern, and the other to fend them off from the high, overshadowing hulls of the big junks. The baby on her back sucked its thumb, silently and without expression, and seemed unperturbed by her jerky movements. After a few minutes they were clear of the junks, and the sampan woman used both hands to propel them along by means of the single creaking oar. She was heading for more open water, but Mitchell stopped her and pointed out the direction he wanted to go. She stopped rowing and looked at him uncertainly.

"No want see harbour — no see floating restaurants?"

Mitchell shook his head, he had no time to play the tourist and take a leisurely cruise around the harbour, and he could clearly see the flamboyant floating restaurants from here. He pointed to the group of poor, tumbledown sampans and said insistently:

"No, tomorrow maybe. Please take me over there."

The woman continued to stare at him, and then decided that it did not really matter where he wanted to go as long as she received her money, and so she did as he asked and rowed in the direction of his pointing finger.

Mitchell directed her to the sampan he wanted, a larger craft draped with washing and with a tumbledown shelter made of old pieces of wooden packing cases built amidships. When the two craft were close he leaned out

244

in defiance of his sampan woman's startled protest, and drew the two boats together. He smiled reassuringly and told the woman to wait, and then stepped into the prow of the larger boat.

An older woman appeared, her face full of wrinkles but in its own way as surprised and uncertain as the younger woman with the baby. Mitchell hoped that this was Jenny's aunt and said quickly:

"I'm looking for a girl named Jenny Peng, do you know where I can find her?"

The old woman looked at him blankly, and then turned to ask bewildered questions of the younger woman in the small ferry sampan still alongside. The two of them exchanged excited words for a moment, and the young woman with the baby made helpless, unknowing gestures with her hands. Mitchell asked his question again, more slowly and carefully this time, but to his exasperation neither of them seemed to understand. The old crone spoke no English, and the younger woman spoke only the few simple sentences necessary for her trade, she could only repeat her offer to show him round the floating restaurants and the harbour.

They were attracting a lot of attention from the neighbouring sampans and Mitchell was beginning to feel foolish. He tried simply pronouncing Jenny's name in the hope of getting some flicker of understanding, but there was no response and he began to wonder if he was on the right boat. More faces were appearing from the seemingly derelict wrecks around them, and finally a Chinese youth with steel-framed glasses stepped uncertainly across the decks of some of the intervening sampans to ask hesitantly:

"What you want?"

Mitchell was glad to find someone who could help, and although the youth did not look over-intelligent he spoke English reasonably well. Mitchell explained his errand, and after a brief consultation with the two women and some of the nearer neighbours the youth turned back to him and said:

"This woman is not the relative of Jenny Peng. You must ask at this sampan over there."

He pointed to another floating hut roofed over with sheets of tin and a faded square of threadbare carpet, and Mitchell again felt discomfited as he realized his mistake. He made his apologies to the still uncomprehending old woman he had first accosted, and then followed the youth as he stepped from deck to deck to reach the sampan he had indicated. An interested audience of old men, women and children watched as he passed, and a black cat hissed at him and almost fell into the harbour in its haste to get away.

Jenny's aunt proved to be another wrinkled old crone, almost undistinguishable from the first, but with the help of the bespectacled youth

Mitchell was able to ask his questions. After interpreting the youth turned back to the young American and said:

"Jenny Peng works at a bar in Wanchai. It is called the *Golden Mandarin*. You will find her there."

Mitchell shook his head.

"No, she doesn't work there anymore. She left yesterday."

The youth looked doubtful, and then spoke to the old aunt again. There was a brief argument of some kind, and then the youth turned back again and insisted:

"She says that Jenny Peng works at the *Golden Mandarin*."

It was enough. Mitchell was convinced that the old aunt knew no more than what she said, and there was no more that he could learn here. He thanked them both and embarrassed by the surrounding poverty peeled a few notes from his wallet in payment. Then he hurried to escape the curious stares he had attracted, and ordered his waiting sampan woman to scull him back to the quayside.

★ ★ ★

Half an hour later he was back in the Central District of Hong Kong and unfolding the whole of his story to Jack Barratt at Eastern station. The Divisional Superintendent listened with his chin cupped in one large hand, and a frown on his weather-hammered face. Barratt had managed to sleep for two four hour periods out of the previous fifty hours and so he felt comparatively fresh. He applied his mind to the disappearance of Jenny Peng, and voiced his only positive thoughts.

"It's a pity that you had to make your own investigations, Lieutenant. If Jenny is under suspicion of having helped us, then your questions at the *Golden Mandarin*, and then at Aberdeen will hardly have made her position any easier."

Mitchell said sharply:

"Maybe — but if I had not gone to the *Golden Mandarin*, then we would still be ignorant of the fact that Jenny is missing!"

"Perhaps." Barratt was not prepared to argue the point. "But we do have that bar under observation now, and it would only have been a matter of time before we became aware that Jenny was not at her job. Then we would have made some more discreet enquiries."

Mitchell was thrown a little off-balance by the rebuke, but he recovered and asked bluntly:

"All right, so maybe I should have stayed away. But now that we do know that she's missing, what are you going to do about it?"

Barratt said grimly:

"For the moment, nothing."

The young American stared at him uncertainly, and then a faint flush spread across his freckled face. The U.S. Navy had taught him not to argue with authority and it was an effort to ignore the rows of silver pips on Barratt's shoulders, but he squared his own back and said doggedly:

"Superintendent, Jenny is in some kind of trouble. At the *Golden Mandarin* they say she's left to find another job, but her aunt doesn't know anything about it and thinks that she is still working at the same place. Everybody stalls me off or just refuses to answer when I try to find out where she's gone, and to me that means that they're lying. Something bad has happened to that girl and it's our fault. You've got to do something about it."

Barratt raised his chin from his hand and said quietly:

"I appreciate your feelings, Lieutenant, and of course you're right. If Jenny Peng is in trouble then we should do something about it. But first we have to face the facts. If Jenny really has disappeared then there are three possible alternatives as to what might have happened to her. One is that Madame Chong has discovered that

Jenny passed that copy of the deathlist on to us, in which case Jenny is most probably dead. Two is that Madame Chong and her Communist friends may only suspect that it was Jenny who helped us, in which case they may give her the benefit of the doubt and keep her alive until they can be certain. And three is that Jenny may have panicked and gone into hiding somewhere."

Barratt had been counting off the alternatives on his fingers, and now he closed the first and third fingers back into his palm again, continuing grimly:

"The first and third we can discount for the moment. If she is dead we cannot help her, and if she has gone into hiding of her own free will then as yet she does not need our help. The middle possibility is the one we must consider. The possibility that Jenny is under suspicion, but is still alive; a prisoner perhaps, but not necessarily in the *Golden Mandarin*. If that is the case then for the police to make any direct enquiries would only improve upon your mistake, convince the Communists that we do have an interest in the girl, and sign her death warrant."

"But you can't just sit there and do nothing!" Mitchell was beginning to boil with frustration again and to him it seemed criminally wrong that Barratt could have endangered the girl and then take her disappearance so calmly. He went on angrily: "They could be torturing her, or preparing to murder her even now. At least you could try to do something — raid the *Golden Mandarin* and search the place!"

Barratt said patiently: "I can't raid anywhere, not even a nightclub and brothel, without a warrant. And to get a warrant I have to have some definite proof that a crime is being, or has been committed. But even that is beside the point. The fact you must understand is that I cannot do anything definite until I know exactly where Jenny Peng is being held. If I were to raid the *Golden Mandarin*, only to find that the girl was not a prisoner on the premises but was being held elsewhere, then I think I could guarantee that she would be dead within the hour."

Barratt paused and then said seriously: "Believe me, Lieutenant, this business worries me as much as it does you. It looks very bad for Jenny Peng, but if we can help her at all we can help her best by doing nothing. Any official move from me would only give the Communists the proof they need to kill her."

Mitchell said harshly:

"They could still be torturing her! God alone knows what they might do to make her talk."

Barratt said softly:

"I'm sorry, Lieutenant. I can't guarantee that they won't torture the girl, but I can be certain that it will cost her life if I allow my C.I.D. force to go barging about like a herd of bulls in a china shop. I'll make enquiries, but they'll have to be made very discreetly."

Mitchell cared nothing that he might be acting disrespectfully now, and said bitterly:

"And you promised her protection."

It was one of those moments when Barratt felt the weight of responsibility crushing all that was good in him, and leaving only the shell that had to maintain the petty façade. There was nothing more that he could say, and there was no comfort in the known fact that disillusionment came to all men in time. He wondered wearily whether there was any real scrap of hope that Jenny Peng would be found alive, and almost inconsequentially whether Marc Mitchell would ever trust another policeman.

15

A Dangerous Game

JENNY PENG was naked except for the gag that was knotted cruelly into her mouth and the tight cords binding her wrists. Two men held her upright before the window of the room that was her prison, and their hands dug like talons into the bare flesh of her arms. They were two nameless, silent Chinese who had been sent by Lee Kung to assist Madame Chong and do her bidding, and they both wore dark trousers and white shirts with neckties loosened at the collar. The man on her left wore spectacles, but otherwise there was no difference between their bland faces. They only smiled when a whimper of pain escaped from behind her gag to show that their rough handling was hurting her, and then their smiles were only a thin flicker of movement across their tight lips.

They had dragged her up from the bed, almost dislocating her arms from their sockets, and there were fresh tears in her eyes as they held her in position at the window. At a word from Madame Chong she was pushed closer so that she could see down into the street. It was early evening and the golden fire was flowing through the neon tubes that shaped the pantomime chinaman sign directly below and to the left of the open window, and in the street below she saw a familiar peaked cap and white uniform. She caught her breath and her body stiffened, for even though he did not look up to show his face she could recognize Mitchell. The Lieutenant's bars were plain on his shoulders, and his slim, boyish figure was unmistakeable. He passed below her, out of sight into the bar, and then she was roughly dragged away from the window again. One man continued to hold her while the man with the spectacles deliberately closed the shutters of the window.

Madame Chong said brutally:

"This is the second time that your American friend has come to look for you, but he cannot help you. This morning he asked questions of Betty Sing, but he learned nothing. Then he paid a visit to your foolish old aunt at Aberdeen, but there again he learned nothing. After that he went to visit the police. There was a man following him throughout the day."

Jenny had choked back a muffled sob, and now turned her eyes to the evil old woman in black who stood just behind her. Madame Chong still held the black leather whip in her hand and Jenny cringed and felt again the open cuts and weals that lay across her burning, naked back. Madame Chong smiled, a vile sneer that merely gave an added twist to her wrinkles, and then continued:

"But I do not think that the police

258

can help you either. They cannot act without proof, and even if they do decide to raid the *Golden Mandarin* they will find nothing. As soon as Lee Kung has made arrangements you will be moved to a place of greater safety. Within an hour it will be too late for the police to find you here."

Jenny made a futile effort to squirm herself free of the man who held her, but his fingers merely stabbed more deeply into her flesh. The other man grabbed her again and between them they threw her bodily back on to the bed. With the flat and back of his hand the first man beat her across the face, breasts and stomach until she lay almost still, her body wracked with sobs and the salt tears flowing down her face.

Madame Chong watched, and rubbed the mental salt into her agony by saying:

"The American will learn his lesson also. I will have men waiting for him in the alley outside when he leaves the bar. They will teach him that it will be wise to interfere no further!"

Jenny Peng closed her eyes but the tears still trickled through her closed lids as she gave way to despair. She felt sorry for Marc with a C, but most of her anguish was for herself. For in her heart she knew even then that she was not fated to become one of those fortunate few of the bar girls who hoarded their money and then escaped to make a successful marriage. All of her dreams were broken and gone, and the future held nothing but more pain and death.

* * *

Marc Mitchell knew that he was playing a foolish and dangerous game, and one that Barratt would have disapproved. In fact, if Barratt had known of his intentions he felt sure that the English Superintendent would have stopped him, and so he had told Barratt nothing. He knew also that the risk he was taking could prove fatal for himself as well as for Jenny, but it was now less than forty-eight hours before the *Carson City* was due to sail and he knew that he could not leave Hong Kong without attempting something positive to help her. He was sure that she must be in trouble now only because he had betrayed her to Barratt and then persuaded her to meet with the policeman, and that gave him a deep sense of guilt. He had broken a promise to her which preyed on his conscience, and Barratt had also failed in his guarantee to protect her. These factors were on the surface of Mitchell's mind as he entered the *Golden Mandarin*, but there was one final factor which balanced all the others of which he was not fully aware. Subconsciously Mitchell possessed the usual streak of romanticism that was likely to stir in any imaginative young man on his first visit to the east, and in this situation it was practically impossible for him to leave Jenny Peng to her fate. He had to attempt something, however wild and foolish it might be.

The bar had several customers at this hour of evening, and the bar girls were at their usual tasks of making themselves friendly and available. Mitchell checked the laughing faces of the girls without any real hope, but still felt disturbed and disappointed that Jenny was not there. The lights were dim and it took him a few moments to distinguish all the faces in the gloom, and then he moved up to the bar. Betty Sing was sitting on one of the yellow-topped bar stools, chatting to a customer on her right, and Mitchell casually took the seat on her left. She turned and recognized him, and for moment her bright smile seemed to be suspended uncertainly on her face, but then she recovered her balance and said hello.

Mitchell gave her a friendly nod and offered her a drink. Betty Sing hesitated, the uncertainty back on her face, and Mitchell knew that he was cutting out the man who had been talking to her previously. The man looked like a casual tourist, and Mitchell hoped that he would not cause any trouble, for it was important to his plans that he should renew his acquaintance with Betty Sing. The girl stayed undecided for perhaps thirty seconds, long enough for Mitchell to sense that it was not only her other customer that prompted her hesitation, and then she nodded.

"Okay, I drink a whisky please."

Mitchell ordered the drinks, and took care not to look at his rival. However, the other man merely gave a philosophical shrug to indicate that he had not been really interested and then moved away. Mitchell felt faintly relieved that his first hurdle had been overcome so easily, and looked at the girl with a self-conscious grin:

"I'm sorry if I've been rude and broken anything up."

Betty Sing smiled briefly, her teeth

showing very white between the red lips.

"It was no matter. We were only talking, and he was not buying me very many drinks."

Mitchell tried a man-of-the-world smile that didn't really fit, and then the drinks arrived. Mitchell raised his glass of beer and made a toast, and Betty sipped delicately at her glass of amber coloured fruit juice. Her eyes watched him with undisguised curiosity, and Mitchell knew that she was wondering why he had returned. He couldn't get directly to the point of his visit, and so he searched his brain hastily for some kind of conversation. Finally he began to tell her about Philadelphia.

For an hour Mitchell made struggling, irrelevant talk, and during that time drank several more small beers and bought a long line of pseudo-whiskies for the girl beside him. He knew that as long as he continued to spend his money freely she would keep him company, and after a while she relaxed her wary distrust of him and began to play up to him in the usual manner. Her smiles became more suggestive and frequently she allowed their bodies to touch. Mitchell was beginning to feel warm, and when he judged that he had spent sufficiently to comply with the house rules he put his arm around her waist for a moment and suggested with an awkwardness that was not wholly feigned that they should retire to her room.

Betty Sing smiled teasingly.

"Not yet. It is too early. Buy me another drink first."

Mitchell was embarrassed. He felt sure that some of the customers at the other end of the bar were listening, and reluctantly he bought more drinks. Betty did not move away from his encircling arm, but allowed her fingers to brush his thigh in a calculated flirtation. They exchanged smiles as she sipped at her new drink, and despite himself Mitchell found unwanted sex thoughts cutting across the purpose in his mind. He knew that the girl meant to play him like the panting fish he pretended to be with all her blatant, prostitute's art, and that added frustration to his embarrassment. He groped for more inane small talk until her glass was almost empty, and then persisted hopefully:

"Shall we go now?"

"Maybe soon." She leaned forward and gave his cheek a promissory kiss. "Just a few more drinks."

She pushed her empty glass confidently across the bar, but before the barman could reach towards them Mitchell had closed his own hand over the glass and brought it back. Betty looked at him doubtfully and he smiled and said:

"I'll buy a bottle of whisky and we'll take it with us — is that okay?"

Her hesitation was only momentary, and then she returned his smile with an assenting nod. Mitchell knew that the bottle would cost him dearly, but he also knew that only by balancing up the money she would have squeezed out of him in time and single drinks would he be able to get her upstairs without any further delays. His previous knowledge of bar girls and bar rules was limited to his experiences with Jenny Peng, but at least Mitchell had an observant mind. He ordered and paid for the bottle, and then Betty Sing took his arm and led him unobtrusively through the golden curtains to the left hand side of the bar.

They went up the familiar flight of stairs to the second floor, and as they passed the small room where he had been entertained by Jenny Peng Mitchell had to resist the sudden, almost over-powering urge to burst open the door and see whether or not she was inside. He checked it because if she was not there and he disturbed some other girl with a customer then the odds were that he would start an uproar that would end with him being thrown out, and then all his fine plans would come to nothing. Controlling the impulse, and suppressing the vivid mental pictures of Jenny being possibly tied and gagged to the bed inside, he continued to follow Betty Sing. She stopped at an identical door further down the corridor, and invited him to enter an identical room, furnished as simply and briefly with just a bed and a small bedside table that held two glasses and a syphon of soda water.

Mitchell went inside, and the close intimacy of the room that was almost filled by the waiting bed caused his heart to beat uncomfortably fast. He put the whisky bottle down upon the table as Betty Sing closed the door, and then he turned to face the girl. She came to him smiling, put her arms around his waist and stood upon tip-toe to let him kiss her offered lips. He kissed her awkwardly because it was expected of him, and had the feeling that this was all horribly unreal. They were repeating almost exactly all the actions he had performed with Jenny Peng. When the girl pulled away she smiled at him knowingly, and then presented her back to him so that he could pull down the zipper of her dress.

Mitchell put his hands upon her shoulders, and his tongue fumbled for words. She turned her head to look at him enquiringly and then he said:

"No, Betty. I don't want to make love to you. I want something else."

Suspicion darkened her eyes, and she said abruptly:

"I don't do other things — only make love!"

Mitchell realized his blunder and explained hastily:

"I don't mean anything like that. I mean that I just want to talk to you." He tried to draw her towards the bed. "Sit down and listen to me for a moment."

Betty resisted him, standing stiffly, and her face was now a cold, uncertain mask. She had discarded the first, automatic conclusion that he was asking for some form of perversion as quickly as it had been born in her mind, but now all of her original fears and doubts were back in place he said slowly:

"We have talked in the bar. Why did you come here?"

"Because I want this to be a private talk." Mitchell pulled out his wallet and offered her a one hundred HK dollar note. "Look, I'll pay you just the same, but you don't have to make love. Just sit beside me for ten minutes and listen to what I have to say."

Betty Sing stared into his face for half a minute, and then at the note in his hand. Dubiously she reached out to accept the money, and Mitchell smiled gratefully and sat down on the edge of the bed. Betty played with the note, folded it, and finally put it away in a small purse. Then, still with some reluctance, she came and sat beside him. She sat a respectable distance away and kept her eyes on his face.

Mitchell said. "It's about Jenny Peng. I know she's in bad trouble and I want to find her. I think that perhaps you can help — "

"Jenny Peng has left this house," Betty interrupted quickly. "I know nothing!"

"Okay, okay!" Mitchell put his hand on her arm as she started to get up from the bed, holding her firmly and hoping that she would not decide to struggle or scream for help. If she refused to hear him out it would ruin everything, and he hurried on:

"I know that you don't know anything now, but you can find things out for me. And if you help me to find Jenny I'll pay you two hundred dollars — not Hong Kong dollars, but two hundred U.S."

Betty stared at him uncertainly, but although she did not relax she did not attempt to pull any further away. She said at last:

"But Jenny Peng has gone to another job. That is all."

Mitchell shook his head. "It's not as simple as that."

It was his turn to hesitate now, but he had come too far to turn back. He was gambling with largely unknown cards and the stakes were high, but he lowered his voice and said carefully:

"I know that Jenny is in serious trouble because she helped the British police. Jenny found out that Madame Chong has been working with the Communists. She told the police and that is why she has disappeared. I think that Madame Chong or her Communist friends are holding Jenny a prisoner somewhere, and that perhaps they will kill her. I cannot help her alone, but you can ask questions of the other bar girls and perhaps find out what has really happened. If you can do this for me, then I'll pay you the two hundred dollars."

Betty Sing continued to stare at him, her face now blank of any emotion. Mitchell swallowed hard, for by now he no longer had to pretend to be nervous and out of his depth. He said earnestly:

"I'll make it four hundred — no five hundred dollars. That's a lot of money just for asking a few questions, more than you can earn in a long time in the bar."

For another half minute Betty remained blank and silent, her arm trembling slightly under Mitchell's hand. Then she asked warily:

"How can I be sure that you have so much money?"

Mitchell smiled at her, partly to put her at ease, and partly because her response was even better than he hoped. He felt that he had already proved himself a naïve and gullible young fool, and to that end he had deliberately placed Jenny Peng even further in jeopardy. Now he lied shamelessly and as convincingly as possible to maintain that impression, and also to stress that despite his worldly simplicity he did have a certain value in other fields.

"I can find you the money," he assured her. "I may be only a Lieutenant but I get pretty good pay. My job is with guided missiles, and that's a very complex and responsible job. The U.S. Navy spent three years and several million dollars to train me in electronics and missile control, and that means that they have to trust me with a whole mass of top secret facts and figures — some of the missiles that we handle aboard the *Carson City* even the Captain doesn't know about. A job like that carries high pay, well above that of the ordinary Lieutenant."

He paused there, feeling that he had said enough for her to remember, and then repeated again:

"The money's okay. The big question is will you help me?"

Betty thought slowly, her face blank and impassive. Finally she raised her eyes to look at him again, but he could read nothing in their narrow depths. She said cautiously:

"Perhaps if you come back tomorrow."

"You mean that you will try and help me?"

"Perhaps. I will promise you nothing. But I will think. For five hundred U.S.

dollars perhaps I will ask the questions for you. But you must come back tomorrow."

Mitchell smiled and accepted the bargain.

★ ★ ★

When he left the *Golden Mandarin* some ten minutes later Mitchell was tensed and half expecting to be attacked. However, Madame Chong had been listening from her position by the concealed peep hole from the next bedroom, a possibility that had not been included but hopefully desired in the young American's plans. The old woman did not have to wait for Betty Sing to faithfully report all that had passed, but she needed time to think. She was satisfied that Mitchell would return and that the opportunity would come again, and so she called off her dogs for the night and allowed him to leave unharmed.

16

Sweet Whisky

MARC MITCHELL returned to the *Golden Mandarin* again on the following night, and the intervening twenty-four hours were hours of almost continuous, sleepless worry. By confirming to Betty Sing, and to anyone who might have been listening in to their conversation, that Jenny Peng had in fact betrayed them to the police he had taken a terrible risk. He knew that Barratt's logic, and his carefully explained reasons for showing no immediate and obvious interest in the missing girl were perfectly valid, but still he considered his actions a necessary risk. His frankness had been rash stupidity, except that he needed to maintain the appearance of a fool if he was to succeed in the devious scheme that was in his mind. The risk that Jenny, if she was still alive, might be killed out of hand the moment that the '*benefit of the doubt*' as stressed by Barratt had been removed, had to be taken, and Mitchell could only pray that at the same time he had provided a new insurance against Jenny's death. He prayed that Madame Chong had swallowed the bait in his talk of missiles and secrets, which was a total fabrication for there were no guided missiles aboard the *Carson City*, and that Jenny would be kept alive as a possible lever for extracting more detailed information. It was all a blind balancing of mental subtleties and responses, as sure as playing chess in the dark, and Mitchell was well aware that the minds of his enemies would be more accustomed to twists and double-thinking than his own, but still he intended to play the game to its finish.

When he entered the bar he looked hopefully for Betty Sing, and saw her almost immediately at one of the tables with another bar girl and two sailors. His heart began to pump the blood a little faster in his veins, for he realized that this, if any, could be the single moment of truth. If Betty Sing ignored him it would mean that the fish were too shy of the tasty bait that he had dangled before them, and if they refused to bite they had no more reason for keeping Jenny Peng alive. He moved towards the bar, and as he passed the table where Betty was sitting she looked up. Mitchell felt suddenly dry in the throat, but he shaped a smile and said:

"Hi, Betty. Are you going to have another drink with me tonight?"

Betty faltered, and for one sick, empty moment he thought that she was going to refuse. Then she turned an apologetic smile to the sailor beside her and said:

"The lieutenant is an old friend — will you excuse me?"

The sailor gave Mitchell a hard look,

but he was out-ranked and finally shrugged his shoulders with ill grace. Betty squeezed his hand and promised:

"I send you another girl, as pretty as me."

She stood up and accompanied Mitchell to the bar. They passed one of her colleagues who was sitting alone, and Betty inclined her head meaningly to the table she had just left. The girl understood, smiled, and went over to make up the party of four once again. From behind his back Mitchell could hear the sailor making caustic comments to his friend about the cheek of wet-eared, frigging officers, and hoped that the new girl would keep him quiet.

They seated themselves on two of the yellow-topped bar stools once again, and Mitchell began once more the endless charade of buying drinks. He had to make empty conversation again, but after a few minutes the barman had to move down to serve a customer at the opposite end of the bar, and

Mitchell lowered his tone to risk a tentative enquiry:

"Did you talk to the other girls?"

Betty looked frightened for a moment, and pressed a finger to her lips. She made sure that the barman had his back firmly towards them and then whispered:

"Not here — we talk later in my room."

Mitchell nodded, and for a moment her behaviour made him wonder whether she might have done the very thing that he had least expected her to; and that was to do exactly as he had asked her, nothing more and nothing less, in the hope of earning the five hundred U.S. dollars he had blandly offered. If that was so then it would throw all of his present plans out of gear and he would have to improvise as he went along, but for the moment there was nothing he could do but restrain his impatience and wait. The chatter and laughter of the bar flowed around them and they added their own unnecessary voices to the general babble. Making the pointless conversation was even more of a struggle tonight, but Mitchell had to persevere because it would have looked odd to have simply sat there in waiting silence. Once he glanced back to the sailor whom he had robbed of Betty Sing's company, and was relieved to see that the man had switched his attentions without too much difficulty to the new girl whom Betty had sent over to his table. At least there would be no trouble from that quarter.

An hour passed, and Mitchell hoped that that was enough. One of the other bar girls had already disappeared with a bashful young sailor from some small town in Kentucky, and that was a good sign. Mitchell touched Betty Sing's arm and suggested that it was time.

She nodded: "Okay, but you must buy another bottle of whisky to bring to my room."

Mitchell didn't argue, although the bottle of the previous evening had remained unbroken, and it was most probably the same bottle that he was buying for the second time now. The barman smiled briefly at the transaction but made no comment. Betty took the bottle and again they went upstairs. She took him to the same room and closed the door, and this time she made a point of locking it.

Mitchell sat on the bed, leaving a space for her to sit beside him, but Betty busied herself with breaking the seal on the whisky bottle, and pouring a one-inch measure into one of the two glasses on the bedside table. She turned towards him with her bright smile, but now there was something fixed and brittle in the curve of her lips as she said:

"We have a little drink first. Do you like soda water in your whisky?"

Mitchell hesitated, he didn't want the whisky but as a sociable gesture he nodded. Betty Sing held the glass to the syphon and splashed a little soda water into the whisky, and then she filled a glass purely with soda water for herself.

"I have already drunk too much," she explained. She sat beside him and handed him the whisky glass. Her own she raised to her lips and said, "cheers!"

Mitchell smiled and raised his glass, but he didn't drink. Instead he asked: "What have you found out?"

Betty looked uncomfortable, and for a moment stared down at the bed.

"I am not sure. I talk to some of the girls like you want, but nobody knows what has happened to Jenny Peng. Perhaps I will try some more."

Mitchell was disappointed, although in this direction he had expected nothing. He pulled a wry face and was thoughtful for a moment. Betty Sing watched him, and then moved closer. She touched his arm, stroking it gently with her fingers, and when he looked at her she was smiling uncertainly.

"Maybe this time you make love to me," she suggested: "We have drink first and then I show you a good time." Her hand moved to caress his leg, and then rubbed meaningly over the front of his trousers.

Mitchell swallowed hard and removed her hand, and then she raised her glass, continuing to smile as she sipped again at her soda water. Almost automatically Mitchell raised his own glass, but he paused again with the rim touching his lips. Betty Sing's bright smile had not changed and her eyes revealed nothing, but in that moment Marc Mitchell had aged into sudden understanding. He knew what was expected of him, and he knew that this time her act of seducing him was purely a blind. His heart began to flutter, and slowly he sipped the drink she had mixed for him.

The whisky had a faintly sweet taste, blurred by the soda water but definitely not the taste of unadulterated scotch whisky. His brain was quite calm and he guessed that the barman had received explicit instructions regarding which bottle he was to be given, and he remembered that Betty had been careful to pour the drinks herself so that he had no chance to inspect the seal. He smiled at her and took a good taste. This was all part of his general plan, and there was a secret elation within him that more than balanced the fast undercurrent of fear.

Betty played her part with him until he had finished his drink, and then she took the glass from him. Three minutes had passed since he had first tasted the drugged scotch, and already he was feeling dizzy. Her laughing smile seemed to magnify before his eyes, expanding and expanding into a vast nightmare of white teeth and red lips, and then the blackness began to descend and he painfully closed his eyes. His body tilted very slowly to one side and he would have fallen on the floor if the girl had not pulled him back. She allowed him to roll the other way on to the bed, and by that time his senses had flown and he was helpless.

★ ★ ★

A minute passed, during which Betty Sing lifted the young Lieutenant's dangling legs and stretched them out more tidily on the bed, and then a sharp knock sounded on the door. Betty unlocked it and stood back quickly as Madame Chong came inside. The old woman walked over to inspect their limp victim, and then chuckled deep in her throat:

"You have done well." The unfamiliar note of praise came easily with her good humour. "Now you can go back to the bar and carry on your work. You are not necessary now."

Betty Sing nodded and hastily left the room. As she went out she passed two waiting Chinese in the corridor. She knew vaguely that they had been sent by the tall man from Canton who had stayed for a brief time in one of the upper rooms, but that was all. She only suspected that they, together with Madame Chong, knew the answers to all the questions that Mitchell had asked, but it was not wise for her to ask those questions. She knew better than Jenny Peng that a bar girl should mind her own business, and so she hurried quickly and thankfully back to her usual tasks in the bar below. Behind her the two Chinese answered Madame Chong's call for assistance and entered the open door of the small bedroom. The door closed softly behind them.

* * *

Thirty minutes passed before a large laundry van appeared in the street outside the *Golden Mandarin* and stopped opposite the entrance to the side alley that led round to the back of the premises. A thin Chinese in blue overalls got down from the cab and began to give directions to the driver. The laundry van backed up slowly into the alley mouth with only inches to spare between the steel sides and the brick walls. As the van backed further inside the thin man had to move one or two rubbish bins out of the way, but slowly the van crawled backwards until it halted a few feet from the rear entrance to the nightclub.

The thin man stared for a moment along the unlit alleyway, which continued until it opened out on to another street, but nothing moved in the silent darkness. If he had walked a few yards towards the second exit he might have tripped over the body of a sprawling drunk who lay against the wall reeking of cheap whisky, but he did not bother to make a close inspection. The smell of the alley made him wrinkle his nostrils and he clearly felt no desire to linger. He went up to the back entrance of the nightclub and knocked carefully on the door. After a moment it was opened, and there was hurried conversation in low voices.

A minute passed, and then two more men appeared, struggling with a large laundry basket that appeared to be awkwardly heavy. The two men were both Chinese wearing dark trousers with white shirts and loosened neckties, and one of them wore plain spectacles. They were silent except for subdued grunts, and the slight bumping and scratching sounds as they carried the large basket out to the waiting van. The thin man in the blue overalls gave them some help, and between the three of them they pushed the basket through the opened doors of the van. The two Chinese climbed quickly in beside it, and the man in the blue overalls closed and locked the van doors.

Another figure moved from the lighted doorway into the nightclub, and spoke curtly to the man in the overalls. The newcomer had the thick figure of an ageing woman and wore a stark black dress. A thin bar of light from the doorway showed her cold eyes and the few wrinkles across her forehead. The man in the blue overalls nodded obediently to what she had to say, and then hurried to catch the van that had already started to move forward. When the van had emerged from the alley the last man climbed into the cab, and then the van drove swiftly away.

Madame Chong glanced around the alley once but saw nothing to alarm her. The stale alley smells had reached her nostrils also, and with an expression of distaste she went back into the *Golden Mandarin*. As the bar closed behind her darkness and silence once more mingled with the atmosphere of dirt and urine. After a while a cat prowled into view, but with animal instinct avoided the inert body of the drunk Chinese.

★ ★ ★

It was almost half an hour before the still figure showed any signs of recovery, and then he stirred very slowly into life. He sat up and shook his head dizzily, and then stared for a long moment at the empty whisky bottle that still lay under his outstretched hand. With an expression of disgust he pushed the bottle away, and then with halting movements and the help of the wall he pulled himself to his feet. He leaned against the soiled brickwork for another long moment, using the wall for support, and then he tottered unsteadily along the alley way, still groping along the wall with one hand until he came out into the street.

He turned away from the neon sign of the *Golden Mandarin*, and in the crowded street he was jostled several times as he stumbled along the pavement. A few of the passing Chinese smiled as they saw his dazed appearance and caught the last of the whisky fumes from the stains down the front of his white sweat-shirt, while others hurried past and pretended to ignore him. The man continued to walk unsteadily until he turned the next corner, and then abruptly his back straightened and his pace quickened.

Sergeant Weng Ki was more than a little disgusted by his own aroma and appearance, and he hurried to make his report to Eastern station before he was picked up and arrested by some of his own colleagues in uniform.

17

The Concrete Cave

WHEN Mitchell awoke he was feeling very cold and uncomfortable. His mind was still dulled and it seemed as though a thick sea fog had penetrated into his head, muffling his senses and clinging shroud-like to every shred of brain tissue. A shiver ran through his body and he tried to reach for a blanket. Something harsh pulled at his wrists, and he began to realize then that he was not waking up in his bunk aboard the *Carson City*. There was a queer taste in the back of his mouth which he vaguely associated with the after-effects of a hangover, and then he began to remember Betty Sing and the peculiar flavour of the whisky she had given him.

He opened his eyes and a little of the fog cleared inside his head. He made no conscious effort to think, but gradually became aware that he was lying partly on his face and partly on his side on a concrete floor. He was cold because he had been stripped naked, and his arms were stretched out in front of him to a point where his wrists were lashed with thin rope to a large iron ring set in the concrete. All this registered, and then after a long moment he pulled himself up a little to make a wider inspection. He saw then that he was in a large, bleak cellar, perhaps twenty yards square. There was one closed door, and a single powerful electric light bulb hanging from the white ceiling. Apart from himself the cellar was empty, just a bare, concrete cave, presumably underground, that could have been anywhere in either Hong Kong or Kowloon.

Mitchell wriggled himself into a sitting position, and shivered again as the damp concrete pressed against a new area of his bare buttocks. His situation looked hopeless and he stared almost with anguish around his empty prison. He had expected something like this, and yet this was more than he had expected. The cave-like cell and his wrists lashed to the iron ring fitted roughly to his preconceived ideas of what he would find when he recovered consciousness, but he had not expected them to remove all his clothes. To reduce a prisoner to nakedness was a good psychological move, for a naked man in modern civilized society felt automatically more vulnerable and helpless than one who was clothed. Also he was a creature open to ridicule, which was equally as damaging to his spirit. Mitchell was no exception and found his own nakedness embarrassing, it undermined his courage and unsettled his tenacity of mind.

He began to wonder how much time had passed since he had drunk the drugged whisky, but there was no way of guessing. They had taken his wristwatch away as well as his clothes, and so he might have been unconscious for any number of hours. There was no way of even knowing whether it was still night or day.

He was able to think straight now, although his head was still a little bit muzzy. He tugged tentatively at his wrists but the ropes binding them were knotted very tightly, and the iron ring was securely bedded in the concrete. He could have pulled and twisted until doomsday, but it was very unlikely that he would ever snap those ropes or wrench the iron ring out of the floor. There was no point in fraying the flesh off his own wrists, and so he did not try. No other course of action offered itself to his searching mind, except the possibility of shouting to attract some attention, and all that he achieved during five minutes of concentrated thought was a growing numbness in his bare bottom where he sat on the hard floor.

He had almost decided to shout and demand attention when the initiative was taken away from him. There was the sound of a key turning in the lock and then the cellar door swung open. Mitchell twisted round to face it and instinctively drew his knees up in an effort to conserve some semblance of modesty. He had never before seen Madame Chong, but he guessed the identity of the old woman in black almost immediately. The man who preceded her into the cellar was an unusually tall Chinese in a western suit, a man whose face and bearing seemed to be stamped with a callous rigidity. Mitchell could not imagine this man bending or relenting from any purpose that he might fix in mind, and he felt another shiver that was in no way connected with the dampness of the cellar running up his spine. It seemed to start from his tailbone and lightly touched every vertebra as it rushed up to settle in a strange chill around the back of his neck.

Lee Kung came into the room and stopped, staring down at the young American with a thin smile just turning the corners of his mouth. Mitchell almost felt the cold examination of those unblinking eyes, and he was acutely conscious of his helpless nudity. Lee Kung's gaze made him want to squirm, and he could feel a flush spreading through his freckles and up to the roots of his crew cut hair. Lee Kung's scrutiny was worse than the casual, disinterested gaze of Madame Chong who stood impassionately by his side.

Mitchell remembered that he was playing a part, and that it was important to let them under-rate his intelligence if he was to take the full advantage of any opportunity that came along. In the back of his mind was the horrible feeling that perhaps he was the fool he pretended to be, but he refused to let that thought take any definite shape. He said hoarsely:

"What's this all about? Why have I

been brought here? And where are my clothes?"

Lee Kung ignored his questions for the moment, continuing to merely stare until Mitchell reddened again and made a futile attempt to attain some more dignity in his sitting position on the floor. With his wrists tied low it was impossible for him to even straighten and square his shoulders, and so the movement caused him to lose rather than gain face. Lee Kung allowed himself a quick, scornful smile, and then made a condescending answer:

"You are here, Lieutenant, for two reasons. One is that we wish to thank you for confirming our belief that it was the girl Jenny Peng who betrayed us to the British police. At first she had refused to admit her guilt, despite the severe whipping she received from Madame Chong. But then we were able to tell her that you had betrayed her in turn, and after that she broke down and confessed. We know now that she found a copy of the deathlist we had circulated, which had been mistakenly included in with some letters she had been entrusted to post by Madame Chong. We know that she foolishly kept that list and then gave it to you, and that you in turn took it to the English Superintendent at Eastern police station. And we also know that later you arranged for her to meet with the Englishman and one of his Chinese lackeys at Aberdeen. Jenny Peng has made a most complete confession, and now she has been sentenced to death for her crimes. My comrades who attended her trial were unanimous on that point."

Mitchell cursed the tall man with a string of hot obscenities which he did not normally use, but which he had overheard frequently on the lower decks of the *Carson City*. The words were in character, and also at the moment they matched his feelings. Lee Kung heard him out with no change in expression, and although Mitchell had automatically tensed himself to receive a kick or a blow none came. By refusing to be provoked Lee Kung left the young American feeling even more helpless and hopeless than before, a fact of which the Chinese was well aware.

Mitchell became silent, glaring from one to the other of his tormentors. Madame Chong had her arms folded across her chest, and although her eyes burned through him she showed no particular inclination for any verbal torture. Mitchell switched his gaze back to Lee Kung who was so obviously in command, and demanded:

"You said two reasons — what was the other?"

"That too is quite simple." Lee Kung smiled gravely and regarded his victim with casual malice: "In the *Golden Mandarin* you talked to a girl named Betty Sing about your work aboard the American aircraft carrier. You are a guided missiles officer, and you boasted rather foolishly of knowing certain secrets that are even forbidden to your Captain. I would be interested to know more about those secrets, and the nature and range of those missiles aboard the *Carson City* — and in fact any details which you may care to tell me about your ship and its capabilities."

Mitchell said tartly:

"You can go and boil your fat head!"

"On the contrary, we might boil yours." Lee Kung stroked his jaw thoughtfully: "You give me ideas, Lieutenant. Can you imagine what it would feel like if I were to have your head immersed in a bucket of scalding water. As painfully effective as thumbscrews, or slivers of bamboo under your fingernails, or so I would think. It would be much more sensible if you simply became talkative again."

Mitchell said slowly:

"I could tell you nothing anyway. There are no missiles aboard the *Carson City*, that was just talk to impress the girl." He was speaking the truth now, but he knew that they would not believe him.

However, Lee Kung studied him uncertainly for a moment, as though some instinct was giving him faint cause for doubt. Then he said coldly:

"We shall see. If you have anything worthwhile to tell us, then you may rest assured that we shall extract it from you. And if not I think that perhaps we can make some good propaganda out of you; a captured war criminal who has taken part in some of the vile atrocities committed by the Americans in Vietnam will make good propaganda. Before we execute you we shall ensure that you sign a full confession."

He turned abruptly on his heel and started to leave, and Mitchell said sharply:

"What's happened to the girl? Where is Jenny?"

Lee Kung regarded him again with interest, but it was Madame Chong who chose to answer:

"Jenny Peng is alive, but only because I prefer to kill her slowly. It was very stupid of her to work against me, and now she truly wishes that she had never been born."

Mitchell winced at the naked cruelty in the old woman's words, and then Lee Kung added with more calculated irony:

"Surely, Lieutenant, you did not think that we would be careless enough to place the two of you together?"

It was exactly what Mitchell had hoped, and it showed in his crestfallen face. All his plans had been to that end, the desperate hope that if the Communists could be tempted to kidnap him in turn then at least the two of them would be held together. He had felt certain that once he could find Jenny, then he could rely upon his own wits and resources to find some way of setting them both free. He had had all the confidence of youth in his own ability to fight, talk or bribe their way out, but now that confidence was abruptly shattered. They were keeping him apart from Jenny and he could not even be sure that she was being held in the same building, and abruptly his spirits gave way to despair. He bit hard at his lip and then Lee Kung laughed. The tall man turned away, signed to Madame Chong, and they both left the cellar. The door closed behind them, leaving Mitchell in dejected misery, and the key turned sharply in the lock.

In the corridor outside Lee Kung stood still for a moment, thinking hard and ignoring both Madame Chong and the silent Chinese he had posted to guard the door. The tall party man knew that killing Jenny Peng was not going to absolve him in any way from the merciless accusations of failure that he would have to face when he returned first to Canton, and then to Peking. The party simply did not accept nor tolerate failure. He could only plead that he had arrived too late to change the course of events and hope to deflect the worst of the fury of castigation on to the heads of the local organizers here in Hong Kong. It was a flimsy hope and one that would need some measure of success somewhere on his side to tip the balance. There was just a chance that a propaganda victory, or a few useful naval secrets twisted out of Marc Mitchell might save him from total disaster, and so he had allowed himself to be influenced by Madame Chong when she had reported the young American's indiscretions and suggested that he might be a useful prize.

Lee Kung knew that the old woman's thinking paralleled his own, and that she too was hoping to redeem sufficient of her own skin to enable her to continue in her present position in Hong Kong. Petty espionage was her specific task, and a small triumph in that field would probably clear her with the iron-willed but practical men in Peking. Mitchell had fallen into their hands like one ripe plum in a particularly barren harvest, but now Lee Kung was beginning to think that perhaps he had fallen too easily. It was impossible to guess at what might have been in the young American's mind, but something in Mitchell's manner had given Lee Kung the uneasy feeling that perhaps he was not lying when he maintained that his talk of missiles and secrets had been merely a bluff to impress Betty Sing. If that was so then there would be nothing with which to impress Peking, for the higher party men could not be so easily fooled.

Lee Kung was troubled, but at least one thing was certain in his mind. If there was to be any more failure then he would revenge himself by killing the American as well as Jenny Peng, and any blame he would transfer squarely on to the scrawny shoulders of Madame Chong. For the moment circumstances had made the old woman his closest ally, but it was a partnership for which he had no relish and he meant to break it as soon as it was humanly possible.

Still pursuing his thoughts Lee Kung eventually walked on down the corridor, and Madame Chong followed him with the usual glitter of hatred in her eyes. She could guess with psychic accuracy at the trend of his thoughts, and she knew that the tall party man would bear a close watch.

The Chinese guarding the door of Mitchell's prison watched them move out of sight, and then cautiously relaxed.

★ ★ ★

At Eastern station Jack Barratt sat at his desk and slowly drank his way through a large cup of black coffee as he waited for more reports to come through from the scattered members of his specially formed ghost squad. He had been off-duty and sleeping beside his wife when Weng Ki had made his first report, but the news had been important enough for Chan to call him immediately. Grace had grumbled a little as he disturbed her to answer the telephone, but she was only half awake and he had managed to get out of bed, dress himself and move softly out of the bedroom without waking her fully. Then he had hurried down to his car and driven fast back to the station.

Weng Ki was waiting to repeat his story, still looking disreputable and smelling of alcohol. Barratt reflected that when the Sergeant played a part he played it to perfection, but there was no time for compliments and he listened closely to Weng's account of the night's events.

The Sergeant had been assigned to watch the *Golden Mandarin* because he was by far the best man that Barratt had available for the job. He had reported Mitchell's first visit the previous night, a fact which had caused Barratt some concern, and he had been watching when Mitchell returned again to make his contact with Betty Sing. The whole business had been as puzzling to Weng Ki as it had been to Barratt, but he knew as instinctively as the Superintendent that the young American must be playing some reckless game of his own. It seemed inevitable to the Sergeant that Mitchell would come unstuck, and instinct had told him that it might be more useful if he kept his observations to the rear entrance rather than the front of the nightclub. Accordingly he had sprinkled himself with whisky, staggered unsteadily into the alleyway just in case he was being observed, and then collapsed in a suitable position for keeping watch.

He explained about the heavy laundry basket which had been carried out an hour later and loaded aboard the large van. The laundry basket had been large enough to contain a man, and it was a suspiciously late hour for any ordinary collection or delivery. Weng Ki was as efficient a policeman as he was an actor, and as a matter of routine he had made a mental note of the registration number of the van.

Chan had already radioed the number

to their patrols out in the streets, and so they could only wait. It was just possible that Marc Mitchell might have emerged unharmed from the front entrance of the *Golden Mandarin* while Weng Ki was doing his impression of an alcoholic in the back alley, and so Barratt checked by radio-telephone with the *Carson City* to enquire whether the young Lieutenant had returned. The answer, as he expected, was negative.

Now several hours had passed, and it seemed that the laundry van had vanished almost as swiftly as it had appeared into the night streets of Hong Kong. The patrolling mobiles reported no sign of it. Weng Ki had been dismissed and had gone to clean himself up and catch some sleep, but Barratt remained awake and reluctant to return to his own broken night's rest.

He was drinking his third cup of coffee when there was a brief knock on his door and Chan entered. His

Senior Chinese Inspector looked calm and unruffled as usual, neither night nor day, nor heat nor riots ever seemed to make any difference to Chan's tidy appearance. Now he was smiling and Barratt recognized a bringer of good news.

"Well, Charles?"

"A report has just come in from the man we had keeping observation at the headquarters of the General Workers Union," Chan said cheerfully: "They seem to have had a busy night as usual, with a large number of doubtful characters both coming and going. Several vehicles made calls to the back entrance, and two hours ago a laundry van passed inside. It was an unusual hour of the night for a laundry delivery, and so our man underlined the registration number on the list he was keeping."

Barratt said thoughtfully:

"The same van that Weng Ki reported at the *Golden Mandarin*?"

Chan nodded.

"But there's more. Half an hour after the laundry van had arrived a taxi pulled up and a woman entered the building. The description fits Madame Chong."

18

Moment of Decision

AT eight o'clock in the morning Barratt attended a hastily called conference that included the Police Commissioner, his three fellow Divisional Superintendents, the Colonial Secretary and the Secretary for Chinese Affairs. They were a serious-faced group of men, and the problem that Barratt had set them gave them cause for much deliberation. Throughout the past three months they had walked a dangerous tightrope in their decision-making, balancing the need to control the violently rioting Colony against the grim fact that any single mistake might be sufficient to release wholesale slaughter in the streets, or provoke a determined invasion by the unleashed masses of Mao's Red Guards clamouring along the line of the frontier. So far they had avoided any drastic mistakes, keeping their heads and refusing to be led into the blunders that had given the Chinese their much-vaunted propaganda victory over neighbouring Macao, and they had no desire to make such a blunder now. Barratt had outlined the facts surrounding the kidnapping of Marc Mitchell, and asked for the authority and a warrant to raid the headquarters of the General Workers Union, but they were reluctant to give him the go-ahead.

The Secretary for Chinese Affairs put the counter argument into precise words.

"Is it worth the risk, Superintendent? So far we have given the Communists very little in the way of provocation, even though they use the word unceasingly, and now there are definite signs that the Colony is returning to normal. Most of their energies and resources have been spent and have failed, and there have been no new outbreaks of violence for the past two days. At this stage it would be folly to give them any excuse to start a new wave of demonstrations."

Barratt nodded. "I appreciate that aspect, sir — but we've known for a long time that most of the organization behind the actual rioting has stemmed from that Union building, and now that we have a cast-iron excuse to make a raid we have a good chance of putting them out of business. I know that some of the momentum has already gone out of the riots, but that doesn't mean that they won't start up again as soon as they get their breath back. If we can break up just one definite centre of subversion, now, while they're weakened and exhausted, then we should be able to throw the whole thing out of gear for good — or at least for a long time to come."

The other men around the conference table weighed his words carefully, and it was the Colonial Secretary who spoke next:

"We must always keep in mind that this is a propaganda game that the Communists have been playing, and if we do make a raid on that Union HQ and fail to find conclusive and undeniable proof that it has been a centre of criminal activity, then we could give them the propaganda victory that they need. A raid on the Union can be interpreted as suppressing the Union, and that in turn means suppressing the workers and people's rights. It's exactly the kind of thing that they want us to do, and some of those hard-core union and party members are almost certain to fight to the death to provide martyrs for their cause. We have to use extreme caution."

The Police Commissioner nodded, but he was not unsympathetic with Barratt. He said slowly:

"We know that they're guilty as hell, John. But can we guarantee that we'll find the evidence to prove it?"

Barratt said grimly: "The evidence

must be there. It's impossible to organize riots on the scale of the past few months without leaving any traces. Unless I miss my guess we'll find the place full of home-made bombs and anti-British pamphlets. But again that's not the point. I'm certain that they are holding Lieutenant Mitchell inside, and possibly the missing bar girl, Jenny Peng. Once we release those two we shall have all the justification we need."

The Colonial Secretary said bluntly: "But can we be sure that the American and the girl are inside. Your Sergeant saw a laundry basket being loaded into a van behind the *Golden Mandarin*, and another of your plain-clothes officers observed the same laundry van entering the union premises, but that doesn't add up to concrete proof that the American was inside the laundry basket. That's just a probable fact that we have to assume. And if we are wrong — "

He left the last sentence unfinished,

and hanging over the conference table like a dark cloud.

Barratt drew a deep breath, and knew that he was going to have to fight every inch of the way to get the decision he wanted. His rugged face set stolidly as he said:

"Nothing is certain, sir — everything in life holds some element of risk. I'm convinced that Lieutenant Mitchell is being held somewhere inside that building, and we *know* that it has been the nerve centre of all our troubles over the past months. But I can't give you a one hundred per-cent guarantee that nothing will go wrong, nobody can do that. I can only say that its a risk with all the odds in our favour, and one that we should take. I'll stake my job on it.

"So far the Communist bosses have all been pretty smug. They know that for political reasons all of their main strongholds are practically untouchable. We know that the Bank of China, and the offices of the *People's Daily*, as well

319

as all the larger union buildings, have all been busily engaged in causing chaos and terror throughout Hong Kong, but we haven't been able to do a single thing about it. Until now! And now, by taking Mitchell inside one of their main subversion centres, they've given us what is perhaps the only opportunity we'll ever have to hit them right where it hurts. And I don't think we should miss that chance!"

The Superintendent in charge of Barratt's neighbouring division said quietly:

"John's right. So far we've only been able to take steps against the rioters in the streets, the poor devils who are just a mob of underpaid tools. But this is a heaven-sent opportunity to strike back at some of the organizers behind the riots — to show them that they're not totally safe and infallible. If we can bring it off then there's a good chance that they won't be quite so eager to whip up more riots in future, regardless of what Peking wants."

There were two more nods of agreement, and Barratt knew that the other Divisional heads were with him. Their hands had been tied too long where the real leaders of the mobs were concerned, and they were prepared to take the small element of risk.

The two politicians still looked worried. The Colonial Secretary looked around the faces of the four police officers and admitted:

"I'm still not very happy about it."

"Neither am I." The Secretary for Chinese Affairs played unconsciously with his pencil and broke the point on his blotter. He laid the pencil down and said frankly:

"I can understand how you men feel. You've done a magnificent job, and you've shown magnificent restraint. But now it really does appear that the emergency is almost over, and it would be a terrible irony to relax that restraint and make the mistake we have avoided for so long." He paused and shook his head. "I really don't know that it's worth the risk."

Barratt said grimly:

"There is another factor, sir. If we don't take that risk then it's almost certain that we'll be condemning Lieutenant Mitchell to death. I don't know why the Communists decided to kidnap him, perhaps he was merely getting too inquisitive about the girl, but I feel sure that unless we make some positive move to help him, then we shall eventually find his body floating face down in the harbour."

The Colonial Secretary frowned, and said:

"It sounds as though the boy's a bloody fool, but we can't disregard him entirely because of that." He paused and then looked at his colleague. "The fact that the boy has been kidnapped does make it more strictly a police matter. Our police forces haven't failed us yet, so I think perhaps we should trust them again."

The Secretary for Chinese Affairs

hesitated, and then gave way.

"All right, I'll go along with that."

The Colonial Secretary turned to the Police Commissioner and said:

"We won't interfere with any decision you make. You know your own job best."

The Commissioner nodded silently, and then looked at Barratt.

"All right, John, you'll get your warrant to make your raid. Take as many men as you need from the neighbouring divisions, and I'll see if I can lay on the army to throw a cordon round the area. I want as many men as possible on this job so that it can be done quickly and with the minimum room for mistakes. Before you go in make a last check with the aircraft carrier to make sure that Mitchell hasn't reappeared, and then time your raid for tonight as soon as it gets dark."

19

Night Raid

IN his concrete prison cell Marc Mitchell lay flat on his belly with his arms drawn underneath his chest so that he could apply his teeth to the ropes that bound his wrists to the iron ring set in the floor. The damp concrete was giving him the ague, and already he felt that he must have contacted double pneumonia, but he ignored his bodily discomfort and worked doggedly at his set task. The ropes were tough, but the taste in his mouth and the occasional shreds of frayed hemp that he had to spit out meant that at least he was making some progress. It might take him hours, but given the time he was sure that he could gnaw his way through.

His moves after that were more than

vague, for he could guess at nothing of his surroundings beyond the cellar, and he had no idea of where he would have to look for Jenny. He only knew that he meant to try. During the past twenty-four hours he had been totally ignored, except for that one visit from Lee Kung and Madame Chong, and he guessed that they were deliberately leaving him in suspense and allowing him to starve in order to break down his resistance. However, they had to come back to him sometime, and he worked his jaws furiously to be ready when that happened. His teeth ached and his mouth was sore, and he could taste blood mixed in with the loosened fluffs of hemp which meant that his gums had started to bleed. He had been biting at the ropes for over an hour, and he only wished that the idea had occurred to him earlier.

★ ★ ★

From outside his cell the Chinese guard watched him with calm amusement through a concealed peephole in the door. When the American had succeeded in freeing himself the guard would call for more help and then they would go inside the cellar and tie him up again. Then they would watch the funny joke for the second time, and perhaps even a third time before the foolish American realized that he was merely wasting his energies.

★ ★ ★

It was eight-thirty p.m. when Barratt made his final call to the *Carson City*. The situation was unchanged and Lieutenant Marc Mitchell had still failed to return, and with that assurance Barratt began to issue his orders. He had his own four mobile Land Rover patrols, plus two more borrowed for the occasion from the neighbouring division, and he lectured the six crews of sturdy Chinese constables, each with a Sergeant in charge, in the wide parade yard behind Eastern station. Chan stood beside him, calm and neat, and with his right hand resting casually by the revolver on his hip.

Barratt's briefing was explicit. The Police Commissioner had been as good as his word in enlisting the aid of the army, and during the past thirty minutes a company of Welsh guards had been swiftly moved across the straits from their barracks in Kowloon. They were now waiting in their vehicles in the large car park beside the vehicular ferry under the command of a Lieutenant Colonel, and waited only for Barratt's order to move into position. Their task was to move in behind the police forces and surround the area while the police forced an entry into the Union building. Barratt detailed three of his Land Rovers, a detachment of twenty-four men, to make an assault upon the rear entrance to the building under the command of Chan. Simultaneously he intended to lead the remaining half of his force through the front doors. Two fast police cars with additional men were detailed to cover the two side entrances to the building, and ensure that nobody used them to escape. The large police vans necessary for hauling away the anticipated flock of arrests were to move in immediately behind the attacking forces. They were the only vehicles that would be allowed in or out through the cordon of soldiers.

The briefing took fifteen minutes, there were a few questions to be cleared up and then additional rounds of ammunition were issued for carbines and revolvers. The order was no martyrs for the Communists, but Barratt was also determined that there would be no martyrs to the order. He expected a stiff resistance and so his men were in full riot kit. Chan inspected them and their equipment and pronounced himself satisfied.

Barratt nodded, and checked his watch, and then ordered them aboard their vehicles. To lead this raid he was using his own official car, and he reached in through the open window to switch on the car radio and pick up the microphone. The voice of the Lieutenant-Colonel waiting with the Guards came through immediately. Everything had been pre-planned and discussed during a second lengthy conference that had taken place during the afternoon, so only the briefest communications and acknowledgements were necessary now. Barratt said calmly:

"Superintendent Barratt speaking. This is zero. We're moving now."

The army man's voice came back briskly:

"Understood. We'll be right behind you. Zero and out."

Barratt switched off the radio and got swiftly into his car. The waiting driver started the engine and Barratt nodded to the attentive constable who stood by the gates. The gates were hauled open and the big police car flashed out of the yard with an accelerating snarl and the eager convoy swirling up the dust close behind. At five second intervals the fleet of Land Rovers and the following vehicles sped out into the street and roared away to the east.

Barratt set a fast pace, for he knew that the army convoy would be moving just as swiftly after his zero hour call. The army vehicles had just the slightly longer distance to travel, but even so their synchronized convergence on the union headquarters made no allowances for delays. The whole raid had been precisely timed and along both approach routes Barratt had more of his constables posted to sort out in advance any tangles of traffic.

However, the assault went without a hitch. The convoy sped through the crowded streets with a total disregard for red lights and the normal traffic controls, with alert police constables at every danger point to smooth their way. Barratt had switched on the siren that was fitted to his car and its high-pitched howl gave them clearance as they rushed through the night. A blur of startled, neonlit faces stared at them as they passed, backing away hastily from the edges of the pavements, but they were through so swiftly that there was no time for any kind of hostile response.

As the union building appeared before them Barratt's driver braked to a stop immediately before the steps leading up to the wide double doors. The first three Land Rovers screamed to a halt behind them with the Chinese constables scrambling fast into the road. Chan's contingent flashed past without a pause and hurtled at top speed round to the back of the building. Barratt already had his revolver in his fist and was leading his men in a rush up the main steps, but their arrival had not caught the men inside wholly by surprise. There had been two watchful Chinese stationed at the doors, and these had quickly withdrawn and slammed the doors in the faces of the advancing police.

Barratt hammered his fist on the door and shouted a command to open it up. The order was ignored, and the doors were of heavy steel and looked unassailable. Barratt was undeterred for he had been aware of the defensive construction of the doors, and he quickly rapped out an order to the Sergeant of the leading Land Rover. The man ran back down the steps with two of his men, and a moment later the three of them were struggling back with a heavy oxygen cylinder and the necessary oxyacetylene equipment for cutting through the steel door.

The Sergeant knelt to light and adjust the torch, and then one of the constables handed him a face shield. Barratt and the other men stood back and waited while the Sergeant applied the lancing blue flame to the door beside the lock. Sparks flew, and after a moment the melted metal began to drip. The Sergeant was tight-lipped and tense as he concentrated on his task, and as the seconds ticked away he slowly burned out a ragged-edged half circle around the lock. When he had finished he switched off the torch and stepped back.

Barratt himself moved forward and kicked open the mutilated door.

As the doors flew inwards the waiting constables surged forward, and were met by more than a dozen agitated Chinese armed with steel and wooden bars. Screaming defiance the defenders did not wait to be attacked but instantly joined battle. In a moment all was chaos and shouting confusion, and the raid had broken up into a series of individual scuffles. The constables used their heavy riot sticks as freely as their opponents used their assorted clubs, and the angry screamings became intermingled with howls of pain. Barratt found himself in the thick of the fray with a furious, moon-faced man in spectacles swinging an iron bar savagely at his head. Barratt had his revolver drawn but he was not prepared to use it. He ducked the savage blow and charged forward beneath it to knock the man spinning with his shoulder. As the Chinese staggered Barratt caught the arm that wielded the iron bar, and deftly he cracked the barrel of his revolver across the white-drawn knuckles. The man yelled and the weapon dropped with a clatter, and then Barratt had him by the scruff of the neck and threw him out of the building and down the steps where the large police vans with the mesh covered windows had just arrived. He did not know then that he had just arrested Comrade Hing Lu, the union secretary and one of the chief Communist organizers.

Only a few minutes had elapsed, but already the initial defenders had been joined by a rush of supporters from the deeper recesses of the building. The large reception hallway was a scene of pandemonium and the police were hard-pressed. A coat stand flung at his feet tripped Barratt and sent him sprawling, and then another frenzied union man leapt upon his back. Barratt struggled to rise and then the man was plucked from his shoulders and hauled away. Barratt turned to see Sergeant Fong grimly bundling his assailant through the doorway. More and more of the struggling Chinese were dragged out and thrust or carried down the steps to the waiting vans, and then suddenly the tide turned and the defenders began to fall back. The dishevelled police pressed forward in a ragged line, all except for two fallen constables no longer fit for duty. The front ranks of the cursing, wildly angry union members suddenly broke and tried to escape through the supporting ranks behind. The ensuing mêlée gave the constables the opportunity to make a few more struggling arrests, and then all of the remaining defenders were fleeing back along the hallway, and scattering in frantic search of escape routes.

Barratt led his men after them in a rush, shouting orders that split his own forces into pursuing groups. Each man knew exactly what to do and one by one they forced open the doors of the different rooms and hustled out anyone who had attempted to take refuge there. Barratt left Sergeant Fong to cover the ground floor, and the second floor he gave to the Sergeant and men from mobile two. The third group he led up to the top floor which was quickly searched. An assorted selection of madly struggling union officials were apprehended in a series of desperate fights, and one man was prevented from setting fire to a room stacked high with anti-British posters and pamphlets. Barratt entered the room as the man was in the act of applying a cigarette lighter to a handful of the pamphlets, and rushed quickly to stop him. The man flung away the burning papers and desperately pulled a water pistol from his pocket. He aimed it at Barratt's face and squeezed the trigger, and instinctively Barratt ducked. A squirt of acid sprayed over his shoulder and small splashes of the liquid burned smoking holes in the sleeve of his jacket. The constable who had followed on Barratt's heels was mercifully quick enough to dodge to the other side, and then with justifiable ferocity he cracked his riot stick across the acid gunman's head. The man fell like a stone, and while the constable stood over him with the riot stick poised for another blow, Barratt quickly stamped out the burning papers.

In the other rooms on the top floor they found more of the evidence that they needed to justify their raid, for most of the larger rooms were modelled on school classrooms complete with desks and blackboards. On the blackboards were chalked cartoon diagrams that showed Chinese rioters killing policeman, with written exhortations to the students to go out and do likewise, and in the desks were found more acid-loaded water pistols and parts of home made bombs. In another room they found a large two-way radio set and other broadcasting equipment, plus a radio operator armed with a Chinese-made automatic who had to be shot down by one of the constable's carbines before they could get inside.

The noise was beginning to abate, and Barratt was examining the captured radio equipment when Sergeant Fong suddenly appeared. The mopping up operations were still going on and the peak of the action was over, but Fong's face was bleak almost to the point of ugliness. Barratt had only seen that particularly strained expression on the Sergeant's face once before, and that was after they had witnessed the murdered body of Constable Ho Kin in the hold of the *Célérité*. Fong said grimly:

"I think you should come below, Superintendent. We've found the girl."

★ ★ ★

338

At the rear entrance to the building Chan and his men had forced the doors and penetrated inside almost as swiftly as the main force at the front. They met almost as stiff resistance, but in the narrower corridors at the back of the building there was less room for a full scale battle to develop. A constable by Chan's side was hit in the face by a length of thrown wood and reeled back with blood pouring from a gash over his left eye, but with only the one casualty they quickly over-powered the Chinese who stayed to fight.

Before the raid began it had been agreed that the most likely place for the Communists to hold any prisoners would be either the upper floors or the basement cellars. Barratt had elected to take the upper floors, and so it was Chan who concentrated on a swift search of the cellars. He could hear the shouts and noise as Barratt and his men fought their way in from the main entrance, and so he ignored the fleeing Chinese who scattered for the staircases leading upwards. All the exits were sealed and very few of them would escape. Instead Chan called to two of his men to follow him and ran directly down to the basement floor.

A group of five Chinese rushed at them as they clattered down the steps, and for a moment they were engaged in a savage hand to hand fight. Chan had his revolver holstered, but while working his way up through the ranks he had been the division's boxing champion for two years, and when the need arose he was more than effective with his fists. He knocked one man unconscious with scientific precision and badly winded another with a hard jab to the belly. His constables were no less efficient and those of their attackers who were still capable of running ran swiftly away.

Chan and his two men gave chase down the narrow concrete passage that lay before them, and then abruptly they came to a side turning and were confronted by a man gripping a short-handled axe.

The man wore dark trousers and a crumpled white shirt with a loose necktie dangling low past his waist. His eyes were twin flames of pure hatred behind his plain spectacles and his hands were knotted white around the shaft of the axe which he held high and threateningly above his head. He screamed at them in a torrent of cursing cantonese and the two constables fell hastily back. There was murder written in the fanatical lines of the man's face, and they were not prepared to pit their riot sticks against the axe.

Chan had also been forced to a halt, and now he swiftly drew his revolver from its black leather holster. The man with the axe saw the gesture and abruptly turned and ran. For a moment Chan was blocked by his own men which gave the fleeing Chinese a few yards start, but then he was sprinting in pursuit and calling upon the fugitive to stop. The man ignored him, but was heading down what appeared to be a blind corridor, and momentarily Chan held his fire. Then the man surprised him by stopping abruptly as he drew level with a closed door, which he jerked open and then slammed behind him again as he vanished inside.

Marc Mitchell was still sprawled naked on the floor of the cellar, with his hands still lashed helplessly to the large iron ring. He had faintly heard the filtered noise and violence that was taking place above, and was tensed and wondering at what might be happening. Hope gushed in him as his prison door burst open, and then vanished into sick fear as he saw the man with the axe. He did not know that this was one of the two men who had pushed him into the laundry basket and helped to bring him here from the *Golden Mandarin*, but he could read the man's present intentions in the glittering eyes and the downward swing of the axe.

Mitchell cried out and frantically squirmed away, throwing his head and shoulders as far as possible to one side; and his would-be executioner was so flustered by the white heat of his own rage that the first swing missed. Mitchell lashed out violently with his feet, trying to score a kick in the man's groin, but then the man had recovered his balance and raised the axe again. The heavy blade started to fall, this time directly at Mitchell's head, and then the door was thrown open and Chan stepped inside. The Chinese Inspector already had his revolver levelled in his hand and this time he did not hesitate. The scene inside the cellar was sufficient justification and he fired once, the single shot killing the Chinese with the axe instantaneously, and the impact blasting him away from the helpless young American. The axe missed its mark again and the steel blade rang noisily as it hit the concrete floor.

★ ★ ★

One of Chan's constables produced a jack knife to cut Mitchell free, and during the search of the remaining cellars that was conducted under Chan's direction immediately afterward another constable managed to produce a blanket to cover his nakedness. The uproar that filled the whole of the union building was now beginning to quieten down as the mass of the prisoners were ushered outside and carried away, and finally Barratt appeared. The Divisional Superintendent's face was grim and it was impossible for him to avoid Mitchell's anxious questions. He had to admit that they had found Jenny Peng tied to a soiled bed in another room.

She had been whipped to death.

20

Samurai

LEE KUNG had been fortunate, for he had left the headquarters of the General Workers Union just two minutes before the fleet of police vehicles had arrived with sirens screaming to make their raid. He moved cautiously in from the edge of the pavement and looked back to see Barratt and the first wave storm the main entrance to the point where the doors were slammed in their faces, and then he turned and hurried quietly away. A last retreating glance over his shoulder showed the oxyacetylene equipment being rushed into position to cut through the door, and he cursed angrily. At the same time an open army jeep came roaring down the road towards him and he realized that even now it might be fatal to linger.

He stepped swiftly into a shop doorway and watched the jeep go past. Apart from the driver the jeep contained two officers in the uniform of the Welsh Guards, one a grim-faced Lieutenant-Colonel who occupied the front seat, and behind him a junior subaltern. In their wake followed a convoy of five heavy, green-hooded army lorries, each one filled with troops and swirling past in a roar of noise and diesel fumes. The jeep and the leading lorries turned off in a screech of brakes and tyres at the next left hand turn in order to circle the block which contained the union building, but the last lorry skidded to a halt and a Sergeant with a typical bull-voice bellowed orders that had a stream of armed soldiers tumbling nimbly out of the back to spread themselves out across the road.

Lee Kung began to sweat a little at his second narrow escape, for there had only been a few seconds difference between being trapped inside the cordon and the fact that he had just cleared the net. He eased out of the shop doorway, and then began to run. A sharp welsh voice called upon him to stop, but the tall Chinese simply hunched his shoulders and ignored the order. Behind him an alert guardsman lifted his rifle and glanced enquiringly at his Sergeant, but the Sergeant pursed his lips, and then made a negative gesture of his head. The soldiers had had their orders too on the subject of martyrs, and the Sergeant was taking no risk of shooting down an innocent man.

Lee Kung kept running hard until he was well clear of the danger area, and then the fact that he was attracting too much attention forced him to control his flight and slow his pace to a walk. Already he had crashed heavily into several startled pedestrians, and had created howls of angry lamentations from an old *amah* whose shopping basket he had knocked flying from her hand into the gutter. After escaping both the main raid and the army cordon it would have been foolish to get himself picked up by some ordinary constable on the beat, and so he made an effort to steady his heaving chest and panting heart, and walk normally.

He looked hopefully for a taxi, but although it was not late by Hong Kong standards it was ten minutes before he was able to hail one to a stop. He scrambled inside and told the driver to take him to Wanchai and the *Golden Mandarin*. Then he sat back and fumed with impatience as the taxi sped him through the blur of gaudy shop signs and neon lights.

When they arrived he paid off the taxi quickly and hurried into the bar. He had controlled his breathing and the fast beating of his heart, but his temper and his blood were both hot. He glared around the bar room with its usual complement of available girls and American sailors, and then headed directly for the golden curtains behind the counter. The barman watched him without interference, but beneath his bar counter he pressed the button that rang a warning bell in Madame Chong's room.

Lee Kung hurried up the stairs, past the floor of small bedrooms where the bar girls entertained their customers, and on to the top floor of the building where Madame Chong had her private apartments. He twisted sharply at the outer door handle, but the door was locked, forcing him to knock and identify himself.

Madame Chong answered him from inside, but she made him wait and it was a full minute before she consented to open the door. She wore as usual a black dress, it seemed that black was her only choice of colour, and beneath the coiled bun of her hair her face showed both anger and uncertainty at this sudden intrusion upon her privacy. Before she could speak Lee Kung pushed roughly past her into the living room, and his dishevelled manner warned her that all was not well. She closed the door sharply and turned to face him, demanding harshly:

"What has happened? What has gone wrong?"

"Everything has gone wrong!" Lee Kung practically exploded the words through his teeth, and for a moment he was in danger of becoming incoherent again. Then he swallowed enough of his fury to spit out an account of the police raid and his own narrow escape.

Madame Chong listened without expression, but then nodded and said calmly:

"But this is good. For the British a raid on the union building is a clumsy political blunder. It is the opportunity for which we have been waiting. Now we can accuse the police of victimizing the unions and incite more riots and demonstrations." Her eyes gleamed for a moment. "We have a real chance now to inspire some genuine hate and resentment in the streets, and perhaps bring the British to their knees."

"You fool!" Lee Kung screamed at her: "It is too late. Our main centre of organization is destroyed, and the British will be able to claim full justification for their actions. By now they will have found the body of the girl — the girl you so stupidly cut to pieces with your filthy leather whip, merely to satisfy your own perversion. And they will have found and released the American — he will bring them here!"

Madame Chong stared at him with black loathing in her eyes.

"It was agreed that the girl should be punished, and that she should die. It does not matter who killed her, it was your task to dispose of the body — not mine. And as for the American, that is your fault also. I advised that he be put aboard a junk and taken to Canton, where he could be interrogated properly. It was your decision to keep him at the union headquarters until he had weakened enough for you to interrogate him personally. You hoped to redeem yourself with Canton and Peking, but you have only blundered further!"

"No!" Lee Kung thrust a hard finger against her chest and pushed her back. "It is you who has made all the blunders. It was you who made the foolish mistake of allowing that deathlist to fall into the hands of the girl. Everything stems from that first mistake! It was your fault that the police were warned and that our night of attempted assassinations failed. It was you who killed the girl and it was your stupid idea to kidnap the American. This brothel of yours must have been under suspicion and that is how the police must have traced the American to the union building. Everything that has gone wrong is your fault — and I shall make that fact clear in my reports to Canton, and Peking."

Madame Chong said shrilly:

"Do you think that you can fool the men in Canton and Peking? Do you really think that they are blind and will not see that you are merely trying to save your own skin?"

Lee Kung smiled savagely: "It is not a matter of trying to fool our comrades in China. I shall simply tell them the facts. I think that the British police will be here very soon to raid this place and place you under arrest. Perhaps they will not be able to prove that you murdered the girl, but they will have sufficient evidence on other charges to throw you in jail. And if I were you I would pray that that jail sentence will be a long one — because after that you will be of no further use to our cause here in Hong Kong, and I can assure you that you will then be recalled to Peking to face further punishment there."

For a moment there was silence in the room. Lee Kung's violent tirade had left him momentarily breathless, and Madame Chong was tight-lipped and holding herself fiercely in check. Her small figure was dwarfed by the tall man from Canton but she showed no sign of being cowed. Her hands were clenched at her sides and within her breast all the long, climaxing years of hatred for the whole male sex were focussing into one malignant flame of fury towards the arrogance and enmity of Lee Kung. The party man was too blinded by his own rage and emotions to read her eyes, and turned abruptly to stalk out of the room.

Madame Chong said hoarsely:

"When will you return to Canton, Comrade Kung?"

It was doubtful if Lee Kung recognized the sneer in the word 'comrade' but he turned to answer:

"I shall return immediately — tonight. I will take a bus back into the New Territories and find the girl who brought me here. It should not be difficult. She will lead me back through the culvert to the Chinese side of the frontier, and from there I can demand any transport I need to take me to Canton."

He reached for the door, impatient to get clear before the police forces finished their business at the union building and staged a new raid on the *Golden Mandarin*, but again the old woman's voice stopped him. She said in a strangely compelling tone:

"Wait, Comrade Kung. There are some documents that you should take with you to Canton. Your masters will not be pleased if you allow them to fall into the hands of the police."

Lee Kung hesitated, and then turned to face her. His eyes were sharp and suspicious, fearing that she merely sought to delay him until the police arrived, but it was possible that she might be telling the truth, and that there were documents of importance. He could not take the risk and said abruptly:

"All right, hurry then and get them."

"They are in my bedroom," the old

woman said calmly: "Wait just one moment."

She turned away and passed through the bedroom door behind her, leaving the door partly open. Lee Kung walked back as far as the centre of the room, but then hesitated again. He knew that no man had ever been allowed to pass into that inner sanctum, and a strange feeling of reluctance came over him that would not let him enter. Instead he waited.

Inside the bedroom Madame Chong gazed round for a moment, almost sadly, at the Japanese screen and her Japanese prints. Every other link with her homeland had been severed long ago, but now she knew that she could not change her heritage, and that despite her changed name and her long years in China she was still Japanese. The blood strain of her ancestors flowed in her veins, and her ancestors had belonged to one of the noble warrior clans of the *Samurai*. She turned slowly to the long, curved sword that hung upon the wall behind the door, and now she knew why she had kept it there for such a long time.

Lee Kung called to her impatiently to hurry, but the old woman's hands were calm and steady as she took the sword down from the wall. Her face was again an expressionless mask as she drew the gleaming blade from its long sheath. In her mind there was no thought, and in her heart there was no emotion; there was only purpose. She laid the sheath upon her bed, and then gripped the hilt of the sword with both hands as she called loudly for Lee Kung to come inside.

Lee Kung still felt that awkward reluctance to enter, but he was worried by the delay. Her call tilted the balance of his indecision and he strode forward, thrusting open the bedroom door. He never saw Madame Chong who was poised and waiting on his left hand side. In fact he never saw anything again, and the last sound that he ever heard was the swiftly descending sigh of the samurai blade.

* * *

It was fifteen minutes later that Barratt arrived in the first police car, its siren screaming and the headlights dazzling the crowds on the pavements. The car skidded to a halt before the *Golden Mandarin*, and both the pavement side doors flew open with almost automatic precision. Barratt straightened up from the front seat beside the driver, while Chan stepped out from the rear door. In the far corner of the car sat Marc Mitchell, still stunned and sick at heart, and huddled in pale dejection inside his blanket. Chan quietly advised him to wait and then hurried after Barratt who was already moving through the bar door below the familiar sign of the pantomime chinaman. A police Land Rover roared up out of the night to halt behind them, and Sergeant Fong and his squad of men ran in support of their officers.

There was a sudden hush inside the bar as Barratt and Chan entered in full uniform, the laughter and clink of glasses dying swiftly away. Barratt ordered everyone present to sit still and take no alarm, while Chan moved quickly through the tables to question the barman in a quieter tone. The man answered reluctantly, and Chan looked back to Barratt and nodded meaningly towards the curtained doorway behind the bar. He paused only to warn the sullen barman that he would be charged with obstruction if he dared to press the warning button below the bartop, and by then Barratt was level with him again. They left Fong to post his men and seal off the ground floor as they hurried to the upper rooms.

A frightened bar girl appeared as they reached the second floor, and Chan stopped her before she had a chance to duck back into her room and ordered her to lead them to Madame

Chong's apartments. The girl obeyed, taking them up to the third floor and pointing out the door they required. Chan paused a moment to tell her to wait for them in the passage, and Barratt went first through the door.

A brief survey showed that the living room was empty, but the door to the bedroom beyond was partly open. Barratt walked forward to push it wide, and then stared down at the neatly decapitated corpse of Lee Kung. Chan came up behind him, tightening his lips but making no comment. They both looked up towards the bed where Madame Chong lay huddled in a strangely small black heap. The Daughter of the Horse had followed the custom of her ancestors in defeat, and had disembowelled herself by committing *hara kiri* with the samurai sword.

21

Delayed Departure

IT was three o'clock the following afternoon when the *Carson City* sailed slowly away from Hong Kong, with Lieutenant Marc Mitchell safely aboard. The giant aircraft carrier had been delayed for twenty-four hours beyond her scheduled sailing time by a minor fault in the engine room, and so the young American had been fortunate to find his ship still waiting. The vessel's vast flight deck was a squared lake of silver in the blinding sun, and the creamed swathe of her wake lengthened imperceptibly across the blue waves to push her gently towards the horizon. She was already too far distant for any individual figures to be distinguishable on her deck.

Standing beside a police car parked

near the waterfront were Barratt and Chan, both of them in uniform, relaxing and watching the carrier out of sight. Barratt had one hand shaded over his eyes, while Chan had both hands resting on the bonnet of the car behind him. After they had been standing there a few minutes Chan said softly:

"He is very young. He has time to forget."

Barratt remembered Mitchell's pale face, and the empty haggard eyes as he had gone aboard his ship. He lowered his hand and looked to his Senior Inspector. He said almost as quietly:

"And you, Charles — will you forget?"

Chan shook his head:

"I saw the girl's body. I will remember. Some things it is necessary to remember." He nodded to the mainland and Kowloon, where the white sprawl of the city hid the distant hills that retreated towards China: "Now the Red Dragon growls and retreats, but perhaps it will roar again. We must watch and be ready."

Barratt nodded thoughtfully. For the moment the danger had receded, for the raid on the General Workers Union had been even more fruitful than they had dared to hope, and had led them to four more left-wing centres in Hong Kong and Kowloon. During the morning more raids had been carried out by other divisions of the Hong Kong police force, with Eastern taking a well-earned rest, and each raid had met with total success. From each of the Communist nerve-centres the police had netted a rich haul of loudly-protesting agents and officials, and had uncovered large dumps of weapons and anti-British literature which more than justified the raids. The captured weapons included a few fire arms, fire bombs, daggers, sharpened stakes and lengths of steel pipe, and a whole variety of crude clubs and explosives. Altogether over five hundred arrests had been made, and despite the fact that there had been a few minor riots in the streets to accompany the general upheaval it was now highly hopeful that the Colony would quieten down and return to normal.

However, even though the immediate future offered them a lull there was still the more distant future to consider. Barratt stared out across the straits to the mainland again, trying to form his own opinions but knowing that he would never see fully into the Chinese mind. He looked again to Chan and asked:

"What do you think, Charles — will Peking try it all again?"

Chan shrugged his shoulders, almost as though it didn't matter.

"Who knows? I do not think Peking will risk repeating her mistakes. It is all a matter of face, and when they attempt to humble us and fail they humiliate themselves. China has lost face in this encounter, although perhaps there is a balance because of their success with Macao. I do not think they will attempt the same thing again."

He paused, and then proceeded to demolish his own argument.

"But the Red Dragon is sick; the provinces are breaking apart, the Great Cultural Revolution has ground to a stop, and the Red Guards are beyond control. There is only one sure way to hold together a disintegrating empire, and that is to unite its many internal hatreds against an external danger. The threat of a common enemy makes an excellent binding force, as every politician knows. Perhaps the Americans in Vietnam will provide the focus point that China needs, or perhaps the Russians on her northern borders — or perhaps even the British here in Hong Kong. We are not so formidable as the Americans and the Russians, and in a real war could be very tidily wiped off the map. At the moment our presence here does have its advantages and Peking does not want us totally obliterated, but perhaps it will

become politically expedient to march
the Chinese army across our borders.
"We must wait and see."

THE END

Other titles in the Linford Mystery Library:

A GENTEEL LITTLE MURDER
Philip Daniels

Gilbert had a long-cherished plan to murder his wife. When the polished Edward entered the scene Gilbert's attitude was suddenly changed.

DEATH AT THE WEDDING
Madelaine Duke

Dr. Norah North's search for a killer takes her from a wedding to a private hospital.

MURDER FIRST CLASS
Ron Ellis

Will Detective Chief Inspector Glass find the Post Office robbers before the Executioner gets to them?

A FOOT IN THE GRAVE
Bruce Marshall

About to be imprisoned and tortured in Buenos Aires, John Smith escapes, only to become involved in an aeroplane hijacking.

DEAD TROUBLE
Martin Carroll

Trespassing brought Jennifer Denning more than she bargained for. She was totally unprepared for the violence which was to lie in her path.

HOURS TO KILL
Ursula Curtiss

Margaret went to New Mexico to look after her sick sister's rented house and felt a sharp edge of fear when the absent landlady arrived.

THE DEATH OF ABBE DIDIER
Richard Grayson

Inspector Gautier of the Sûreté investigates three crimes which are strangely connected.

NIGHTMARE TIME
Hugh Pentecost

Have the missing major and his wife met with foul play somewhere in the Beaumont Hotel, or is their disappearance a carefully planned step in an act of treason?

BLOOD WILL OUT
Margaret Carr

Why was the manor house so oddly familiar to Elinor Howard? Who would have guessed that a Sunday School outing could lead to murder?

THE DRACULA MURDERS
Philip Daniels

The Horror Ball was interrupted by a spectral figure who warned the merrymakers they were tampering with the unknown.

THE LADIES
OF LAMBTON GREEN
Liza Shepherd

Why did murdered Robin Colquhoun's picture pose such a threat to the ladies of Lambton Green?

CARNABY
AND THE GAOLBREAKERS
Peter N. Walker

Detective Sergeant James Aloysius Carnaby-King is sent to prison as bait. When he joins in an escape he is thrown headfirst into a vicious murder hunt.

MUD IN HIS EYE
Gerald Hammond

The harbourmaster's body is found mangled beneath Major Smyle's yacht. What is the sinister significance of the illicit oysters?

THE SCAVENGERS
Bill Knox

Among the masses of struggling fish in the *Tecta*'s nets was a larger, darker, ominously motionless form . . . the body of a skin diver.

DEATH IN ARCADY
Stella Phillips

Detective Inspector Matthew Furnival works unofficially with the local police when a brutal murder takes place in a caravan camp.

STORM CENTRE
Douglas Clark

Detective Chief Superintendent Masters, temporarily lecturing in a police staff college, finds there's more to the job than a few weeks relaxation in a rural setting.

THE MANUSCRIPT MURDERS
Roy Harley Lewis

Antiquarian bookseller Matthew Coll, acquires a rare 16th century manuscript. But when the Dutch professor who had discovered the journal is murdered, Coll begins to doubt its authenticity.

SHARENDEL
Margaret Carr

Ruth didn't want all that money. And she didn't want Aunt Cass to die. But at Sharendel things looked different. She began to wonder if she had a split personality.

MURDER TO BURN
Laurie Mantell

Sergeants Steven Arrow and Lance Brendon, of the New Zealand police force, come upon a woman's body in the water. When the dead woman is identified they begin to realise that they are investigating a complex fraud.

YOU CAN HELP ME
Maisie Birmingham

Whilst running the Citizens' Advice Bureau, Kate Weatherley is attacked with no apparent motive. Then the body of one of her clients is found in her room.

DAGGERS DRAWN
Margaret Carr

Stacey Manston was the kind of girl who could take most things in her stride, but three murders were something different . . .

THE MONTMARTRE MURDERS
Richard Grayson

Inspector Gautier of Sûreté investigates the disappearance of artist Théo, the heir to a fortune.

GRIZZLY TRAIL
Gwen Moffat

Miss Pink, alone in the Rockies, helps in a search for missing hikers, solves two cruel murders and has the most terrifying experience of her life when she meets a grizzly bear!

BLINDMAN'S BLUFF
Margaret Carr

Kate Deverill had considered suicide. It was one way out — and preferable to being murdered.

BEGOTTEN MURDER
Martin Carroll

When Susan Phillips joined her aunt on a voyage of 12,000 miles from her home in Melbourne, she little knew their arrival would germinate the seeds of murder planted long ago.

WHO'S THE TARGET?
Margaret Carr

Three people whom Abby could identify as her parents' murderers wanted her dead, but she decided that maybe Jason could have been the target.

THE LOOSE SCREW
Gerald Hammond

After a motor smash, Beau Pepys and his cousin Jacqueline, her fiancé and dotty mother, suspect that someone had prearranged the death of their friend. But who, and why?

CASE WITH THREE HUSBANDS
Margaret Erskine

Was it a ghost of one of Rose Bonner's late husbands that gave her old Aunt Agatha such a terrible shock and then murdered her in her bed?

THE END OF THE RUNNING
Alan Evans

Lang continued to push the men and children on and on. Behind them were the men who were hunting them down, waiting for the first signs of exhaustion before they pounced.

CARNABY AND THE HIJACKERS
Peter N. Walker

When Commander Pigeon assigns Detective Sergeant Carnaby-King to prevent a raid on a bullion-carrying passenger train, he knows that there are traitors in high positions.

TREAD WARILY AT MIDNIGHT
Margaret Carr

If Joanna Morse hadn't been so hasty she wouldn't have been involved in the accident.

TOO BEAUTIFUL TO DIE
Martin Carroll

There was a grave in the churchyard to prove Elizabeth Weston was dead. Alive, she presented a problem. Dead, she could be forgotten. Then, in the eighth year of her death she came back. She was beautiful, but she had to die.

IN COLD PURSUIT
Ursula Curtiss

In Mexico, Mary and her cousin Jenny each encounter strange men, but neither of them realises that one of these men is obsessed with revenge and murder. But which one?

LITTLE DROPS OF BLOOD
Bill Knox

It might have been just another unfortunate road accident but a few little drops of blood pointed to murder.

GOSSIP TO THE GRAVE
Jonathan Burke

Jenny Clark invented Simon Sherborne because her daily gossip column was getting dull. Then Simon appeared at a party — in the flesh! And Jenny finds herself involved in murder.

HARRIET FAREWELL
Margaret Erskine

Wealthy Theodore Buckler had planned a magnificent Guy Fawkes Day celebration. He hadn't planned on murder.